Dry 1

Matt Condon, *The Sun Herald*: Ⱶ
deals with up-to-the-minute issues, complete with contemporary
street, hotel, cafe, bar and personality references, and all wrapped up
in the mantle of a thriller. Cole, a long-time resident of Balmain, has
made the turf her own in *Dry Dock*...Written with clarity and pace,
this is a fine first novel that also laments the loss of suburban values.

Stuart Coupe, *The Sydney Morning Herald*: Cathy Cole's *Dry Dock* is
set around the formerly working class and now increasingly yuppified
inner-Sydney suburb of Balmain. As with the work of Marele Day,
Jon Cleary and Peter Corris, the urban environment of Sydney is very
much at the core of this novel. Private investigator Nicola Sharpe finds
herself embroiled in perceived union corruption and suspect goings-on
involving building developments in Balmain...a highly entertaining
and well-sustained novel from a newcomer.

Skin Deep

Graeme Blundell, *The Weekend Australian*: Reading Cathy Cole's
Skin Deep makes it clear why women writers choose crime over other
literary models in order to explore political structures. And how, in a
rocket ride of visibility, they have given the genre a new lease of life
through the female voice, moving their private eyes from curiosity
pieces to a kind of critical mass in the late 1980s...Cole uses mordant
social commentary to greater effect, resisting hyperbole, pastiche
and the overdone one-liner humour that bedevils many new crime
novelists.

Debra Adelaide, *The Sydney Morning Herald*: Fans of Cole's first
novel, *Dry Dock*, won't be disappointed by the next story involving
Annie Lennox look-alike and medium-boiled PI Nicola Sharpe...
All the right ingredients are here: images of the city as tawdry and
corrupt (and most of its inhabitants not much better); a lone gumshoe

with a beat-up car and handy police connections; vividly drawn locations from Balmain to Glebe and the Easter Show; and a snug love interest to compensate for all the meanness and grubbiness of the world of art fraud and political conspiracy.

Anne Fussell, *Courier Mail*: *Skin Deep* is...a bright and lively read, taking the reader on an intimate journey through the waterside suburb of Balmain alongside private eye, Nicola Sharpe...*Skin Deep* is a great read and Cathy Cole is a welcome addition to the Australian crime family.

The Sunday Times: Cole is a good storyteller who imbues Sharpe with an attractive, distinctive voice and unfolds her well-concocted story at a pleasing pace. The social observations and descriptions of inner Sydney are witty and evocative and the characters ring true. An enjoyable read.

The Examiner: Furiously paced, this Australian crime thriller is an engrossing read...Cole's first novel, *Dry Dock*, was shortlisted for the Ned Kelly Award, and her latest piece is also worth much acclaim.

Christopher Bantick, *The Sunday Tasmanian*: Cathy Cole's first book, *Dry Dock*, was shortlisted for the Ned Kelly Award. Her new crime novel, *Skin Deep*, is one to stop you in your tracks...Cole writes with assurance and insight. She clearly demonstrates a cool facility with the crime form. But the overpowering strength of *Skin Deep* is that it is a cracker of a story.

Catherine Keenan, *Sunday Life*: A fast-paced, Sydney-based, street-savvy thriller...Gripping throughout.

Gold Coast Weekender: Big things are anticipated from Sydney crime writer Cathy Cole, who is being compared to the likes of Janet Evanovich and Sara Paretsky. That's high praise but it is nevertheless well founded.

Private Dicks and Feisty Chicks: An Interrogation of Crime Fiction

Graeme Blundell, *The Australian:* Something for every armchair sleuth and mean streeter. Stylishly shifting between personal observation and critical commentary, Cole entertainingly lifts the lid on the dark world of crime fiction.

The Thrilling Detective: This academic monograph examines the continuing popularity of crime fiction and investigates its ongoing relevance, ranging from socio-economic, feminist, moral and political concerns, but also gets down and dirty (and a lot more fun) when it looks into why some books work and some don't and the origin of the term 'red herring'.

Gabrielle Lord: With insights gained from being both a crime writer and critic, Cathy Cole examines crime fiction entertainingly and thoroughly in this book.

The Grave at Thu Le

Delia Falconer, *Weekend Australian:* By creating a shimmering and enigmatic narrative surface, Cole perhaps mimics the dangerous delicacy with which the D'anyers family has repressed and aestheticised its own colonialism. This sense of elusiveness and fragmentation is strikingly reinforced by the texture of Cole's book. While *The Grave at Thu Le* may at times seem to concentrate too much on beautiful surfaces, this is also a sign of its humility, its understanding that we can sometimes only grasp someone else's past in wispy fragments.

Mark Thomas, *Canberra Times:* Cole's book is an unalloyed pleasure. Vietnamese history has not often inspired foreigners to deeply sentimental reminiscences, except, in its own bizarrely odd way, Marguerite Duras's *The Lover*...The book is sentimental, but not cloying; affectionate, but not indulgent. Cole's overall effect is one of collage, of impressions superimposed on top of each other, of memories juxtaposed with emotions, of sensations experienced one after another to form a palimpsest. Her texturing of text is intensely rendered and most accomplished.

Cameron Woodhead, *The Age*: *The Grave at Thu Le* is a picturesque and evocative novel. A family saga that spans more than a century, it is intermeshed with a lively rendition of Vietnam's turbulent history.

Alison Hetherington, *Herald Sun*: *The Grave at Thu Le* provides an illuminating window into Vietnam's long history.

Drusilla Modjeska, *The Monthly* **(extract):** In its sure-footedness with language, *The Grave at Thu Le* echoes the modernism of Virginia Woolf, or more obviously Marguerite Duras, but it doesn't have Duras's self-absorption, or her slightly repellent self-referential eroticism. If there's an eroticism here it is for the place, an affirmation of the visible, elusive contemporary Hanoi, with the optimism of its young population – two-thirds of whom were born after the war ended in 1975 – working its own curious blend of the global and the communist with ancient traces of the dragon taking flight.

[Cole] writes without the guilt that has been so debilitating to our political and intellectual culture. She doesn't engage with debates about guilt or blame, neither fending them off nor joining the chorus of mea culpa. She brings an awareness to attitudes of mind that Australian readers will recognise, even if the French–Vietnamese history is unfamiliar. It is Cole's probing of nostalgia as a response to the discomforts and displacements of a post-modern, post-colonial world that is the challenge of *The Grave at Thu Le* – and its success.

Jane McLean, *Business Traveller Asia*: *The Grave at Thu Le* meanders slowly, steadily, like a Sunday stroll through a tree-filled park. There are no thrills, no spills, no great revelations, but rather a touching narrative set in a city soaked in a fascinating, yet sometimes, turbulent history.

The Poet Who Forgot

Peter Pierce, *The Sydney Morning Herald*: Cleverly crossing boundaries of genre, Cole's book is arresting from its first moment until its plangent last words.

Christopher Bantick, *The Hobart Mercury*: This is a book that is both subtle and deeply poignant. The book, palpably affectionate in its rendering of Hope, is not panegyrical in tone; Cole avoids eulogising...There is much in this book to enlighten readers about Hope's considerable life. But what lasts is the gift Hope gave Cole. It is how she came to understand herself and through that to discover a kind of love for a man who wrote poems for 50 years and then, she says, 'forgot'.

Kevin Hart, *The Australian*: Catherine Cole met the same man I had come to love a decade after I did, and her new book, *The Poet Who Forgot*, is a fond memoir of her mentor. In 1982, as an undergraduate, she wrote to Hope, whose poems she admired. He exemplified, she thought, the three attributes that Vladimir Nabokov deemed essential to a writer: 'storyteller, teacher, enchanter'. Hope replied to her letter with his usual hospitality, asking her to visit him if she should ever be in Canberra. And so began a lively correspondence, enriched by lunches and dinners spent talking of Louise Labé and W. B. Yeats, prefaced by whisky and lushly extended with red wine.

Geoff Page, *The Canberra Times*: *The Poet Who Forgot* certainly does do justice to the complexity and contradictions of a much-admired Australian poet who almost certainly will remain an important figure in our literature and, indeed, in world literature.

Victoria Laurie, *The Australian***:** Writer Catherine Cole has done something too few of us do. She has taken time out to reflect deeply on a person who helped shape her career and who arguably changed her life.

The Perfume River

Geordie Williamson, *The Australian***:** Attractively produced, carefully edited, and – to my ignorant ear, at least – often beautifully translated, *The Perfume River* is a labour of love that is a credit to all involved in its production. It reminds us of how correct Marcel Proust was, when he said that it is only through the agency of art that we leave our own selves and know what it is to be another.

SEABIRDS
CRYING
IN THE
HARBOUR
DARK

ABOUT THE AUTHOR

Catherine Cole is a writer and academic who lives in Australia, the UK and France. She has published novels, non-fiction, poetry and short stories.

SEABIRDS CRYING IN THE HARBOUR DARK

CATHERINE COLE

UWA PUBLISHING

First published in 2017 by
UWA Publishing
Crawley, Western Australia 6009
www.uwap.uwa.edu.au

UWAP is an imprint of UWA Publishing,
a division of The University of Western Australia.

National Library of Australia Cataloguing-in-Publication data:
Cole, Catherine, author.
Seabirds crying in the harbour dark / Catherine Cole.
ISBN: 9781742589503 (paperback)
Short stories, Australian.
Refuge in literature.

Cover image by Liesbeth de Jonge
Typeset in 11pt Bembo by Lasertype
Printed by McPhersons Printing Group

This project has been assisted by the Australian Government
through the Australia Council, its arts funding and advisory body.

 uwapublishing

For Becky

Contents

Acknowledgements   xv

The Sea, The Sea   1

Forever Restarting   12

Home   24

The Fret   34

Dein ist Mein Ganzes Herz   42

The Remote Lands of Art   54

The Rabbit   64

The Navigator   70

Hell Comes, Hell Goes   84

Love   92

The Rat Inside   103

Salt   113

Some People's Lives   123

Drones   133

Little Kerrie   142

CONTENTS

A Funny Story to Relieve the
Tedium of Reality   152

Going to Visit Dad   165

Steers   177

My American Friend   189

Snakes of the World   198

The Ring   206

Plenty   214

Acknowledgements

A number of stories from the anthology have been published in a variety of journals and anthologies or performed in productions as follows:

'Home' was published in *Meanjin*, No. 69, 2010, and *Best Australian Stories,* Cate Kennedy (ed.), Black Inc., Melbourne, 2011, and was translated into Chinese and published in *World Literature*, Beijing, 2013.

'Dein ist Mein Ganzes Herz' was published in *Sleepers Almanac No. 9*, Sleepers Publishing, Melbourne, 2014. It was produced for BBC Radio 4 by David Roper, Heavy Entertainment, as 'The Road from Austinmer Beach', 18 July 2014.

'Love' was published in *Australian Love Stories*, Cate Kennedy (ed.), Inkerman & Blunt, Melbourne, 2014. It will form a key narrative in the Australian Marriage Equality campaign in 2017.

'The Rabbit' was published in *Animal Studies Journal*, 3(2), 2014.

'The Sea, The Sea' was published in *Ninth Letter*, Illinois, USA, 2016.

Tell her this
And more, –
That the king of the seas
Weeps too, old, helpless man.
The bustling fates
Heap his hands with corpses
Until he stands like a child
With surplus of toys.

The Black Riders and Other Lines, Stephen Crane, 1895

This quiet roof, where dove-sails saunter by,
Between the pines, the tombs, throbs visibly.
Impartial noon patterns the sea in flame –
That sea forever starting and re-starting.
When thought has had its hour, oh how rewarding
Are the long vistas of celestial calm!

What grace of light, what pure toil goes to form
The manifold diamond of the elusive foam!
What peace I feel begotten at that source!
When sunlight rests upon a profound sea,
Time's air is sparkling, dream is certainty –
Pure artifice both of an eternal Cause.

The Graveyard by the Sea, Paul Valéry, 1920

The Sea, The Sea

Lucy Nugent wrote the words THE SEA on the blackboard, on a faint, chalky palimpsest of the previous day's classes.

'Okay,' she shouted, 'how many of you boys have seen the sea?'

'I have, Miss.'

'Have you, Johnnie?' She tried to keep the disbelief from her voice. 'Yes, Miss, on the TV.'

The rest of the kids sniggered. 'Anyone else?'

'We've *all* seen it on TV, Miss.'

'Has anyone really been to the seaside and stood with their feet in sea water?'

The room rustled as the children looked around. They knew no one had been to the coast but they checked in case, for liars, for the too dumb to know the difference between the real world and the television, for the dreamers.

'Right. Let's try to imagine it. I'm going to write some words on the board. One at a time, put up your hand and call out a description, please.'

'Wet, Miss.'

'Good boy, Eric.'

'Blue, Miss.'

'That's right, Ian, but sometimes it can be green too.'

'Is it ever purple, Miss?' Johnnie again. The class laughed more loudly this time.

'Yes, Johnnie, at sunset the sinking sun can turn the water lots of other colours, like orange, red, purple, yellow. It can make the sea look like it's on fire.'

'I've seen a picture of a sunset on the sea, Miss.'

'That's wonderful, Peter.'

'The water would be deep, Miss.'

'It would be, Sam, especially the further you go from the shore.'

'It would be salty, Miss.'

'Correct, Liam.'

There was a pause as the boys sought more adjectives.

'Rough, Miss.'

'Yes, on a windy day.'

'Smooth, Miss.'

'Yes, the opposite, on a still day.'

'Sharky, Miss.'

She sighed. 'What do you mean, Johnnie?'

'There would be sharks, Miss, and whales and dolphins and fish. Tortoises and stingrays like the one that killed Steve Irwin, Miss, because he swam too close and got in its way.'

'The sea is full of marine creatures, boys. Please write down the words. Marine. M. A. R. I. N. E. Creatures. C. R. E. A. T. U. R. E. S. Later we might draw some of them, okay, but first I want you to think about the sea and how else you might describe it.'

She walked to the window and gazed out at the school-yard while she gave them time to think. Heatwaves radiated off the corrugated iron roof of the toilet block. A dust devil spun past the bike racks.

'Miss?'

She turned slowly. 'Yes, Johnnie?' She could see the anticipation in the other boys' body language. They were waiting for a silly question, something typically Johnnie, something not quite of the herd. Johnnie had his hand up, still.

'It must be very old, Miss.'

She tried to keep impatience from her voice. 'What do you mean, Johnnie?'

'The sea must be ancient to get that big, Miss.'

Lucy saw a vast stretch of blue, a millennium of stories flowing with it, the sea as ancient as Ulysses, Vikings, armadas, sea battles, fleets and fleets of explorers, boat people.

Eric put up his hand. 'What's the difference between a sea and an ocean, Miss?'

She turned his question around to the class. 'What do you think, boys? How would you answer Eric's question?'

Johnnie's hand shot up. Lucy looked to the other side of the room, willing another child to reply. 'Yes, Tom,' she said at last, ignoring the chopping impatience of Johnnie's arm.

'An ocean is bigger and a sea is closer to land.'

'Very good, Tom. Who would like to add something to that?'

Up Johnnie's hand went again. Just then, a bell resonated through the classroom's prefabricated walls. It was time for playlunch and the boys began to stand.

'Sit down for a moment. Sit down! Geography homework for tomorrow. I want you to draw a picture of the sea

3

as realistically as you can. Eric! Tommy! Did you hear me? Right. For tomorrow, lots of lovely colour and detail. We'll pin them up and each of you can explain what you've drawn.'

When the boys had gone Lucy set about tidying the room. Arithmetic was next and the transition between subjects was important if they were to concentrate on the new lesson. She removed all traces of the sea from the room – some library books, a map and a small plastic globe. She tidied each boy's desk, picking up any rubbish and putting it in the bin. That done, she went to the window again. The boys were hurling themselves around the playground. Some played tag, others kicked a football to each other. She looked for Johnnie but couldn't see him. She took her mug from the drawer in her desk and a neat pink fuji apple, then went to the staffroom to make a cup of tea.

The school's two other teachers were there before her, Miss Elwick, who was the girls' teacher, and Mr Howe, who managed the older boys.

'Hello, Miss Nugent,' Mr Howe said as she came in. 'Ready for a cuppa?' He reached over and switched the electric kettle on. 'Shouldn't be too long. It's only just boiled.'

Lucy smiled and went to the sink to rinse out her cup. She found it silly that the teachers addressed one another so formally but it was what the parents expected, or so Mr Howe had told her when she first arrived.

'Having a good morning?' he asked.

'Not bad.' She looked across at Miss Elwick, who was buried in the newspaper – probably looking for a new job, Lucy thought. Who could blame her?

'My lot were restive,' Mr Howe said. *Restive* was one of his favourite words. He made his students sound like a herd of buffalo or steers. He'd grown up around here so that made sense. More cattle than people.

'We've been doing geography. The sea.'

'The sea, eh? That'll come in useful in these parts.' He bent double at his joke.

'They need to know about the world beyond their own,' Lucy said.

Mr Howe chuckled on. 'Should we teach them the difference between a surfboard and a cow?'

Miss Elwick looked up from her paper. 'Some of them might want a better life, Mr Howe. Some might even want to go to *university*.'

Mr Howe chuckled. 'Say that when they're through high school. Most will be needed for their parents' farms or businesses. They'll be lucky to get past Year Nine.'

Lucy took her tea outside. The older boys from Mr Howe's class were gathered in a far corner of the yard. Were they smoking? Surely not. She started to walk towards them.

'Miss?'

'Yes, Johnnie.'

'I've got a seashell at home, Miss. I can bring that in tomorrow.'

Lucy took a sip of the tea. 'Really, Johnnie? That would be very useful to our discussion.'

She'd already been wondering where to gather some props. She could print some pictures from the internet tonight; she had a couple of library books about the sea. She might even bring in some of the tins of fish she had at her motel unit: sardines and tuna, the tuna tin specially marked 'dolphin friendly'. That might spark some interesting discussion.

Johnnie was regarding her intently.

'What is it?' she asked.

'My father's got one of those fish that sings and wags its tail. I could bring that too.'

She had no idea what he was talking about.

One of the older boys had seen her coming and the group separated like curdled milk, one lot going into the toilet block, the others towards the basketball court.

'Sorry?'

'It's got batteries, Miss, and it sings.'

She realised he was talking about the kitsch singing fish that had reached town a few years after its popularity had waned in the city. 'Oh, right. Don't bring that but do bring the shell. Okay?'

'Okay, Miss.' Johnnie ran off and Lucy went back into the kitchen.

'I think some of your boys are smoking in the toilet block, Mr Howe.' She washed and dried her mug.

Mr Howe looked at his watch. 'Bell's about to go. I'll catch 'em at lunchtime.'

At four, Lucy packed up her room and walked the few yards to the motel where she was billeted. The afternoon was still hot and a dry wind was stirring the red dust. A flock of budgerigars had landed in one of the ghost gums by the pub and they chattered and called to one another, a yellow, blue and green crowd against the stark contrast of the gum's white branches. She stopped to admire them. Nothing had diminished her wonder at such things. Only a few days ago she'd walked down to the near-empty creek after work and been startled by the screams of a pair of black cockatoos. When she'd looked around for the source of their agitation she'd seen a wedge-tailed eagle soaring high above them, brown and wide-winged in the hard blue sky.

She kicked off her shoes and spread out on her bed. The air conditioner droned. When the evening was cooler she'd go for a walk, have an early dinner at the pub, then she'd prepare tomorrow's class with the TV on. But she slipped into a heavy sleep, from which she woke befuddled, the smell of the rough bedspread in her nostrils, the crisp cold breath of the air conditioner on her head. The sky had darkened and through the open venetian blinds she could see cars pulling up at the pub and men getting out of them. She liked to eat early to avoid the boisterous, man-filled bar, but it was late now and she had no choice but to tidy her hair and brave it. She could always ask for her food to be takeaway, she decided. She'd return the plate tomorrow on her way to school.

She needn't have worried. Mr Howe was in the dining room with his wife, Elaine, and when they saw her they called her over and insisted she join them.

'I was saying to Bill only the other night how we never see you in here, love,' Elaine said.

7

'I usually eat early,' Lucy said. 'The motel room's got a microwave if I want to heat something up.'

Elaine clicked her tongue. 'That's no way to live. You and Miss Elwick should come out to us. I'll make you both a nice dinner. You can't eat on your own all the time.'

'Thanks,' Lucy said. Her steak arrived and she dipped a chip into the tomato sauce that accompanied it.

'Keep the local farmers happy, that's what I say,' Mr Howe said approvingly, towards the meat.

The next morning Lucy packed her bag with the tins of sardines and dolphin-friendly tuna, and a menu from the pub she'd borrowed the night before in an inspired moment when she'd seen the words *surf and turf* on the menu. She hoped it would prompt some discussion about identity and the difference between people who lived by the sea and those who worked on the land. She had her geography books and her pages about the Great Barrier Reef from the internet. She had a page on the First Fleet and a map of Botany Bay and a picture of Bondi Beach shot from above, the people on the sand looking as small as bull ants.

Mr Howe was in the staffroom when she walked in with her things. He looked at the rolled-up printouts, the pub menu in its blood-red plastic binding. She'd explained at dinner what she wanted it for, though he'd seemed sceptical.

'Surf and turf,' he said now. 'They aren't big oyster eaters, these kids.' Again he bent over as he laughed.

Lucy didn't think many of the people around here were. If seafood arrived from the coast it was usually in tins or jars.

The dam offered yabbies, she'd heard one man say in the bar. 'Good with beer. You lure them with a bit of old meat on the end of a string.'

She went to her room to set up the class. She stuck the printouts to the wall and artfully arranged the tins of fish on her desk. She drew down the map and wrote the names of all the oceans on the blackboard. She placed the plastic globe at the centre of her display then pulled a string from one end of the window to the other, tightened it and took some clothes pegs from her bag. In a school with limited resources, you learned very quickly to improvise. She glanced out into the schoolyard. The boys were arriving, the ones who lived in town slouching along the dusty main street, some riding battered bicycles that had been passed down from fathers and older brothers who now worked on the farms. Cars pulled up – utes mostly, some with dogs of uncertain pedigree tethered in the tray. As she watched, the bell rang and the latecomers began to run. The classes lined up, Miss Elwick's girls' class in their yellow uniforms on the far side of the schoolyard by the basketball courts. The boys marched inside. Lucy waited at the door and counted them as they filed past her. Twelve of them, the sons of the local farm labourers, railway workers, people who couldn't afford to send their children to boarding schools in the city, whose children made do with this red-dust education, gathering motes of knowledge to get them through a life of uncertain work, droughts and political indifference a long way from anywhere else.

'Right, have you all drawn the sea as I asked?'

'Yes, Miss.'

There was a rustle as crushed pictures were pulled out of schoolbags.

She walked between the desks to look. 'One by one I want you to hang your picture on the string across the window and explain what you've drawn.'

Starting with the front desks, the boys rose and went to the string. 'This is what it's like under the sea, Miss.'

'This is an iceberg, Miss.'

'My father said there are rainbow fish, Miss.'

'This is a tsunami, Miss.'

'Miss, this is a sunset over the sea, that's why it's orange and purple.'

Johnnie stood and went over to the string. The smallest boy in class, he had to stretch to pin his drawing to the line and as he did so his shirt pulled away from his shorts, exposing the elastic of a pair of grey and grubby underpants.

'This is the sea, Miss. It's got waves and this white stuff is foam.'

Lucy wondered what the boys' parents had made of the exercise. 'How many of your parents have seen the sea?' she asked. Most of the boys raised their hands.

'My parents went to Bondi Beach for their honeymoon, Miss.' This caused a collective giggle.

'My father once worked on a fishing fleet, Miss, off Kurumba.'

For a moment they all looked silently at the blue line of the paper sea they'd created, each page lifting like a live thing in the already-hot morning breeze.

Tears flooded Lucy's eyes. The boys had not yet smelled sea salt, felt the damp kiss of ozone, the roar of waves as they rushed to meet the sand. They were people of the dust, fashioned from the red, dry interior of a country which lacked that other dimension so vital to human life – water – that partnering of sea and land. They had not yet felt the peace that came from the unassailable encounter with a vast ocean. Forget about nations based on land boundaries, she thought, what links us all is our shared origin in the sea.

The boys were whispering amongst themselves, pointing out the details in their pictures. And the pictures really were very, very good. The boys had taken a good stab at something that had come to them second-hand and they had got it right.

'Miss. Miss!'

'Yes, Johnnie.'

He held up a large white shell. It was a conch, perfectly formed, its pointed spire, its white-tinged frill ancient and imposing on the boy's upturned hand.

Lucy gazed at it for a moment before taking it from him.

'My great-grandfather brought it back from the war, Miss. He was in New Guinea, Miss, and he found it on a beach just before he came home.'

She looked at the boy carefully now, at his little damp face and searching eyes, his hair perpetually in need of a comb.

'Well, thank you, Johnnie, for bringing this in. Boys.' She called them to her. She placed the shell against her ear first, a conspiratorial look passing between her and Johnnie. He knew what was coming. Had he done this with his father, his grandfather, perhaps even the great-grandfather who'd found it on a beach on his way home from war?

'It's the sea, Miss,' Johnnie shouted as the other boys clamoured to take the shell and listen too. 'It's the sea, the sea.'

Forever Restarting

Charles rented a house on the cliff overlooking a curve of beach the locals called Horseshoe Bay, though this was not its real name. Somewhere in the bay's curve was a symmetry so perfect the sea seemed to set course for it. The tides rose and fell, high, low, spring, neap, and the waves, like stallions racing across the bruised surface of an ancient amphora, stretched out their heads, their manes in full pursuit, and galloped for it. Standing at the window that offered the best view, he would watch the water doing that thing he'd seen bay waves do elsewhere. It was a kind of zigzagging, something of a warp and weft, as though the pull to shore was resisted by some waves while others sped on. Day in, day out, by moonlight or starlight, the white crests swept steadily towards the centre of the bay's curve, so preposterously driven, even the seagulls seemed impressed.

Often, when he wasn't writing, Charles succumbed to the sentimental urge to listen to music about the sea. It seemed only right to offer something to the sea music outside and its rumble, roar and crash. Elgar, Debussy, some sea songs performed by Kathleen Ferrier, her voice like rich fruit cake, treacly and aromatic. He heard in the notes each composer's search for interpretation, the struggle between the concrete and the fluid, the attempt to capture and still an element made of quick movement, a relentless pull backwards and forwards at the moon's will. He thought he might compose whole sections about it for his memoir, his writing slowing as the days turned wintery and reflective. So many times in his life he had shared something momentous with the sea – childhood, adolescence, middle age – a whole lifetime in conversation with a moving, indifferent thing, infinite and unfathomable. He decided he would start each chapter with a quote about it: the Cornish beaches of his family holidays, a school outing to the Isle of Sheppey, the summer his parents divorced and his mother took him to Corfu, the winter he and Iris spent Christmas at King's Lynn. He might also include his amniotic swim towards birth, his summer baths in a tin tub set under the apple trees, his boarding-school bathing roster: all of them personal annexations of water, the self at its centre.

He had come to Horseshoe Bay at his publisher's suggestion. Walter Stein, his companion through a lifetime of manuscripts and prizes and hints of a Nobel Prize which never came, the shift from fiction to nonfiction in frustration at the ways of making things up. In nonfiction he'd found something ageing, or so it felt at the time, as though certitude was a way of growing up. Biographies, a history of a city, a travelogue of sorts through ancient Greece. 'Write your memoir next,' Walter urged, and in his pleas Charles saw what each morning's mirror offered: an old man's face reflected back. 'Write your memoir, Charles,' it said, 'you are getting close to death.' Walter had even found him this house. A friend's, he said, though he didn't say whose. Charles looked into the family photographs that lined the hall in the hope he'd recognise a familiar face, but none of the people were known to him. He'd come, he told himself, though he knew it to be only partly true, because at some point you must set your life out, lest others beat you to it.

Walter rang every few days to ask how he was going, questions about Charles that were really questions about the progress of his manuscript. 'Not bad,' Charles said, avoiding the specific. He had found that writing a memoir was more about recalling than writing, each new day's thoughts and ideas seasoned by the previous night's dreams. It was as though reflecting back sixty years opened a doorway to impossible ghosts, those spectres bricked into some inner place now released to haunt. He tossed and turned through revisited gaffes and false starts, the shame, the hurt, the moments of cruelty and arrogance. Outside, the sea rose and fell towards the shore. The house shuddered with its pounding. Get up and write, he told himself when he couldn't get back to sleep, but words that enchanted during a restless night turned leaden by morning.

This morning Charles was playing Elgar's *Sea Pictures*, John Barbirolli, Janet Baker, and over a breakfast of marmalade toast and Earl Grey tea he read the record sleeve. Each song from a poem, some known and recited at Charles's old school, his headmaster fancying himself a poet, determined his boys would be able to recite a poem or two. Wordsworth, Keats, W. B. Yeats, the old teacher's favourite was Tennyson's 'Ulysses', each boy a Telemachus who might inherit the explorer instinct of his father or the patience of his mother, Penelope. And Keats's stout explorer, Cortez, in Darien and regarding the sea? As he limbered up to write, Charles wished he could capture something of Cortez's wonder. The sea outside offered no help with that. It rolled and tossed and crested and broke as the days moved along in fractions of tea, toast, a shower, music. A while – he no longer measured the time spent – leaning against the window frame and looking down at the water. This morning, his lips still tasting of marmalade though he'd cleaned his teeth since breakfast, Charles looked at the waves and thought about his first lover, Iris, and how they'd met. She had risen from securing her bicycle in the rack, her arms full of books, her gown damp against the curves of her short, muscular body. She smiled, said something so softly he could only nod uncomprehendingly, and then off she went. A few moments later she came back to the bike rack. 'I've been looking for a tutor. Well, he said he's in Room 104. You wouldn't happen to know that room, would you?' Charles had walked with her up a stone staircase so worn from centuries of feet that each step was as curved as the bay outside and just as treacherous when wet.

Before he went to bed last night Charles had written the words 'When I was sixteen' on his notepad. 'It's a trick of Hemingway's,' an American friend said. 'I know I'm teaching my grandmother to suck eggs, but when you get writer's block, write a sentence to springboard you into the next day's work.' Charles had been looking at his sentence for an hour now and it had springboarded him only to the view outside. As he watched the sea's white horses, those maned curves and crests rushing towards the shore, he heard again the words of Elgar's song cycle: 'Oh! brave white horses! you gather and gallop.' Adam Lindsay Gordon. *When I was sixteen.* Screw Hemingway, he thought. This is like playing charades with oneself.

Iris's Dublin accent was barely discernible. She'd said once, 'Oh, Charles. What is it about you that makes you so sure of yourself?' The roll of the r's, su*rrr*e, sounded very Irish. Had they all been so ambitious back then? Oxford. Black gowned, like ravens they flew on their bicycles down Catte Street. And the certainty, how arrogant they were, so convinced that a place in the world was waiting. Those studying drama as he was, part-time dramatists who spent more time declaiming other people's lines than writing essays, wasted hours talking of how talent scouts would flock to the end-of-year review. The scouts would laugh their heads off and clamour with offers of a part or a play to direct. West End, no doubt, or something suitably lumpen for the BBC. Those fluid dynamics, the ways in which people ebbed and flowed, were buffeted, drawn backwards and forwards, tidal all of us, at study, in love. He saw Iris again, this time at a party in her famous red dress, a clinging jersey that dipped low, exposing the silky abundance of her breasts. She was flirting with one of the dons, lighting his cigarette, softly touching his arm. She walked over to where Charles was standing by the door, watching. 'Oh, Charlie,' she said. 'Come and meet some nice women.' And when he hesitated she touched his arm too. 'You're not queer, are you? If you are I'll just have to introduce you to some nice young men.'

Walter said, 'Everyone wants to know when you got your first big break. The first London production with Olivier.'

'A lot happened between Oxford and then.'

'I know, I know. Tell them about the struggle certainly, but make a lot of all the big names. Olivier, Gielgud. Who was that Australian fellow? Peter Finch? Yes, him.'

And I won't forget Iris, Charles thought, though her fame had waxed and waned since she'd first burst onto the literary scene. For a while there she'd written a book every year. She became more famous than any of her friends and she made Charles famous for all the wrong reasons. He couldn't even maintain his anger with her about that. She'd slipped into a hollow place, no memory, no past, her friends elided as she crumbled and disappeared.

The little rotund clock on the hall table chimed eleven, an insipid sound like a child beating on an empty tin can with a stick. Charles looked at the piles of books on his desk, the bounty of a successful stage career, then an equally celebrated career as a novelist, a nonfiction writer, a commentator, a soon-to-be memoirist. The waves outside rose into sharp little twists, like upended ice-cream cones or those college spires that drew poor old Jude the Obscure to Oxford, the colleges seen from afar, spearing a rook-peppered, tepid grey sky. In his college the wintery rooms smelled of wet woollen pullovers and shoes drying against radiators. Leather and shoe polish and toast and tea.

Iris published her first novel in 1954, when she was thirty-five, in Cambridge by then and still sending Charles letters about her efficiency with rations, though thank goodness rationing was about to end. She had a name by then for lovers, some women, some men, and she'd met John, the compromise choice – the man with whom she'd merge the philosophical with the creative. She was well on the way to fame while Charles was still travelling around the country with amateur theatrical troupes. '*The Good* bloody *Companions*,' he wrote to her from Bradford. 'Please tell me I haven't been trapped in a novel by J. B. Priestley.' He marched the depressing northern city's streets, past cloth-capped men and snivelling children, coal-bruised buildings, the sulphurous smell of the not-so-distant pits, Bradford's factories a'whirr with cotton gins. 'Oh, Charles,' she laughed when he phoned to say he'd at last arrived back in London. 'What an exciting life you lead.'

Fame came for him too, eventually. Stage plays that spoke of the glittering prizes of Oxbridge, an officer unable to settle down after the war, a woman with small children who longed for escape. *The Times* called his work 'the most exciting contemporary plays on the London stage'. After each new production, each new review, Iris called to congratulate him, and with each call he drew their shared summers around him like some kind of dandelion clock. In Oxford, the colleges' stone as yellow as dandelion flowers and brittle with privilege.

They had punted the River Isis, past Church Meadow, Iris trailing her hands in the water.

'Do you really want to direct plays, Charles? Wouldn't you rather write them?'

'I don't want to think about it till I'm through these exams. I swear Sparkes is threatening me with a second if I don't work harder.'

That bell laugh; she splashed water at him. 'You should aim for a third. Far better to fail badly.' The light burnished the college walls, the sun flashed crystal in a mullioned window. She recited from *The Tempest*, her favourite play:

'"Nothing of him that doth fade, But doth suffer a sea-change Into something rich and strange."' She called to some friends in another punt. Teasing, she splashed them as she had splashed Charles. '"O! wonder! How many goodly creatures are there here! How beauteous mankind is! O brave new world, That has such people in't!" You'd cast me as Miranda, wouldn't you, Charles?'

'Of course,' he said. He knew he had no promises to keep. She had been like a dealer to him then, exhorting an addict to try another drug. Had she known that the lure of the play would one day be overtaken by the pull of the novel? Reject those marionettes on stage, declaiming, muttering, falling out above the footlights, manifestations of a life he'd imagined but never lived. But it hadn't been like that really, had it? The war, blackouts, the tired men in damp woollen uniforms that smelled like wet dogs. The looks – he'd seen them all right – of men about to depart for battle while Charles and his friends studied on. He scribbled some notes in his notepad. *Make more of that.*

From stage director to playwright, with girlfriends, wives, mistresses. He lost touch with his Oxford friends, each sloughed like a layer of skin. At first he felt abraded by the loss, and he awaited the new layers as they were sure to come. Regenerated. Transformed. He won awards and famous actors appeared in his work. They put on the masks of all his former selves, his friends, his teachers, the odd notable face illuminated in a darkened audience. How easy it becomes to create characters rather than live with people.

Iris came to London to see his latest play. She could turn heads still, though marriage had filled her out and her hair looked as though it had been shaped by a pudding bowl.

'It's so good, Charles,' she said over a post-play cocktail. The cast were acting up around the piano and he noticed that Larry and Joan had disappeared.

'Do you think so?'

'Yes, I certainly do.'

As she smiled, the glass still at her lips, he recalled the first time they'd made love in his rooms in Oxford. It was hardly successful. She seemed too detached, too cold. He asked her if he was hurting her or whether she'd prefer another position. She replied with a little laugh and with that he finished. They had made love only a few times more. He hadn't the heart for it and he knew she hadn't either. There are friends and lovers, he supposed; some relationships might sit on the cusp for a while but, really, there is no point in forcing either.

The sun outside had reshaped the curve of the bay, adding new dimensions and shadows. Last night he had been searching for a word and it came to him now – bathymetry: the way the depth and shape of the shoreline and the sea floor influenced the tide. He and Iris had influenced each other for a while, her books, her prolific writing, her accolades, her friends. And his. Through the 1950s and 1960s they raced towards success like a myth of some kind, the huntress Atalanta and the golden apples, Hippomenes who eventually won her. Well, John Bailey had won on that front. Then in 1978 a new book was published, *The Sea, the Sea*. To be fair, Iris had spoken to him about it. 'My dear Charles,' she said. 'I hope you like it. I'll get the publisher to send you an advance copy.' They were rivals by then – a Booker nomination for Charles one year, for Iris the next. She sold in droves – 'women's writing,' Walter called it. 'Why don't you write more for that market, Charles?'

This new book was to be her greatest success. It won the Booker but lost her his love. A man called Charles, a lost love, the sea. A pompous and vain man so self-deluded the reader couldn't help but laugh at him. What a fool. What a tosser. A playwright. A stage director. Chatto and Windus sent Charles the promised copy: hardcover, its beautiful sleeve with Hokusai's *The Great Wave off Kanagawa*. He'd opened the book eagerly, lifting its newness to his face to take a great draught of it.

The bay outside was nothing like Hokusai's woodblock. It lacked definition; it was loose around the edges like a scene viewed through rain.

He read the book. He waited for Iris to call. He certainly had no intention of calling her. What would he say? How could you do this? Is this how you see me? Have you hated me all along? Over the next few weeks friends called to chat about anything but Iris's book. They talked of politics, of restaurants and the latest plays. He might have had cancer or been unaware of a sign pinned to his back: *Kick me*. Their silence confirmed what he suspected. They'd all read the bloody thing and they thought he was the Charles of the novel. He might as well drown himself. Get drunk in one of the bars where he and Iris drank cocktails whenever she was in London. He might go on TV to refute her, but it would do no good.

He saw a copy on the sideboard at a friend's dinner party and he lifted the book and showed everyone. 'This picture is quite remarkable, isn't it? See, that isn't a wave in the background as you might think. It's Mount Fuji. Clever to trick the eye with a wave that might be a mountain, or a sacred mountain that might be a wave.'

He was fooling no one. The book disappeared and was replaced with a carafe of claret.

When he heard Iris had Alzheimer's disease he thought at first it might be divine punishment. Everything swept away, everything lost. She would no longer remember him or her books. He remembered her, though, year after year. He couldn't look at the sea without feeling the cruel play of her work. She had loved Paul Valéry's poem, 'The Graveyard by the Sea'. It had inspired her novel's title. As he looked out the window he decided that the poem would provide the title of his memoir too. That sea forever starting and restarting. *La mer, la mer, toujours recommencée*. The sea offered itself to writers so generously. He shielded his eyes, the sun acting like a wartime searchlight. A spotlight made a better metaphor – the playwright blinded as the audience threw rose accolades at his feet.

He went to the cinema in Fulham Road to watch the film that had been made about Iris's life. He sat in the dark by himself. He'd chosen the time of day when no one much was about, just a couple of giggling schoolgirls and a woman who ate popcorn all through the film. Across the darkened cinema he was aware of the rise and fall of her arm as she dipped her hand into the popcorn bucket and then lifted it to her mouth. It seemed a sad, cheap thing to do as Iris's life swept across the screen.

'Are you happy now? Do you realise what you've done to me?' He'd rehearsed the phone calls, the admonishing conversations over drinks. Her blank face. He knew Iris could mask her cruelty. 'What happened to that young woman in the punt who wanted to play Miranda? You are Ariel, my dear, you have created a tempest.'

He stood at the salt-sprayed window. How long had he been leaning on the frame? His arm felt stiff against the hard press of the wood. The afternoon had drawn on, pulling a cloak of twilight behind. It had darkened the water; it was steely now. The horizon had disappeared and soon the land would follow. Across the arc of sand he could just make out a couple of tiny dots. Two people and a third speck, a dog. The people were throwing driftwood for it to chase. They made their way left to right. The wind chopped the waves, drawing night into them in little seismic pulses.

He sat down to write at a desk too loaded with books and scripts and diaries and letters. They had become a burden. He was a drowning man and his books would pull him down.

When I was seventeen and went up to Oxford, I met a woman who would one day make my name synonymous with the sea.

Iris's bare arm plunged into the waters of the River Isis in Oxford. It rose, a long chain of drops along it. She let it fall again and rise. The water settled and unsettled in rings, cracked open and refracted.

Home

Ahmed has rented a house to the west of the city, a stone's throw from Rookwood Cemetery. His friend, Bert, brought him here. As Ahmed's official visitor, Bert brought sweets and books to Villawood. He took Ahmed some new black socks once, and cigarettes, though neither of them smoked. Bert's eyes are an odd blue and when he laughs lines fan from them. There is a gap between his front teeth. 'Now we are *unofficial*,' Bert said on the day of Ahmed's release. And Ahmed nodded, grateful at last to have a friend.

'Nothing special about this place,' Bert said when he opened the front door. 'Fibro. But it'll do till your papers are ready. And it's very quiet,' he joked, pointing at the house's only neighbours: two monumental masons with work yards rarely used, two other dingy houses, the dead.

Ahmed inspected the peeling paint, the large garden at the back, the outdoor laundry. Hiding in Baghdad with neighbours, he'd read old *National Geographic* magazines. London looked very big, Paris elegant. He didn't like the thrusting New York skyline or Singapore's clipped blandness. He was sorry his house was a long way from the wicked blue of Sydney Harbour, the curve of the Harbour Bridge, painted one end to the next over and over, he'd read, as the great Greek Sisyphus had laboured with his rock.

Now he's been in his house a month, Ahmed goes into the city to look at the harbour, returning on silver trains that carry within them the desperate scents of a long working day, of someone's dinner of takeaway chicken or fried potatoes, the callers on mobile phones telling people where they are...*nearly* home, they say...I'm nearly *home*. As soon as he gets home he likes to walk slowly into the cemetery, the visits allowing him time to regain something of himself, some sense of a purposeful past from the rows of neglected graves. Gone are his train trip's greasy takeaways, the sweaty underarms, the plasticine smell of schoolchildren. All is grass and loam, the scent of decay and sun on stone. He often worries that the silver trains run too close to the cemetery for eternal rest, the clatter of the carriages pulsing deep into the earth. In his country the dead are buried beyond a city's walls, where it's quiet, and too far away for the spirits to walk back into town. Here they mingle with the living and a few times now he has seen a phosphorescent haze above his street, ghosts straying beyond the cemetery walls. This is when he feels his difference most keenly. What could he say to these wraiths? In Rookwood, he decides, the steaming souls like to see smiling faces, to gather some happy images of the living world and fortify their darkness. What use are thoughts about rich and poor, migrants and long-ago generations, the venerated whose mausoleums are dotted here and there?

Flimsy or not, the house at least offers a quiet space from which to watch the street pass: the trains slowing for Lidcombe station, the Orthodox church on the other side of the tracks. It is the view from the back of the house he prefers, the garden with its shrivelled old lemon and unpruned roses just like those at home.

He lost his wife Feroza to cancer in 1986. His son and son-in-law were taken away to be tortured one night four years ago. Ahmed and his friends searched everywhere for the boys while his daughter wept into the hair of her newborn son. Then a neighbour came to say he'd seen the bodies thrown into a trench on the outskirts of town. Ahmed had gone looking for the grave but he never found it.

One day, when his daughter finally comes, they will plant basil and parsley, tomatoes and oranges. They will fill the garden, every inch of it, with grapes and figs and plums. And when all their papers are finally approved, they'll find a beautiful house with brick walls and a red-tiled roof and there they'll live in happiness until they too are dead.

Ahmed turns towards the cemetery gates. Walking alone helps to pass the time while he waits for news of his daughter. There are other places he could go, to the big shopping centre in Parramatta or the cinema, but the films are often cruel, the language coarse and brutal. When he buys his groceries afterwards his eyes are still dazzled by the blood and violence. He offers thanks before each solitary meal. Waits. This cemetery gate is always open. Ahmed passes through it and looks across the wide vista, the higgledy-piggledy rows of graves, some with family portraits. The barely discernible mounds of long dead children, the white crosses. Some of the suburb's migrants are buried in this cemetery. Not under this old angel missing one of its wings or an overturned urn, a residue of soil around its lip like ancient coffee grounds. It might yet sprout the pale blue flowers he heard a woman in the Lidcombe fruit shop call 'Easter daisies'.

The migrant dead are in their allotted spaces – the Chinese and Vietnamese, the Jews, the Muslims, the Christians – each group burying its dead in its own way, aligned as their religions decree. A sheet, thin as filo pastry, might lie between the corpse and the earth. Their ashes might have been scattered to the four winds. They are the lost generations of his new city, some long dead, like the doctor from whom this angel perpetually tries to fly, and the woman whose children numbered fourteen, each one of them dead before her. Distant reds and yellows mark the graves of the cemetery's Chinese. He has walked over to that area a few times now, drawn at first by the bright flowers, red silk carnations mostly, some silk roses. They looked like a child's storybook garden in which the flowers always bloom and the sun always shines, round, its beams radiating from a face as smiling as Bert's.

In one *National Geographic* he'd seen pictures of European cemeteries that looked like ancient cities full of houses, temples, cobbled streets down which the living came with guidebooks and cameras searching for the famous. This cemetery is nothing like those but it holds something true about death: the dead must be held in stone. Cats, like the skinny shadow walking slowly towards the old Western gate, must sun themselves on the slabs. The wind must eradicate the names from the tombstones and subsidence must consume the burial mounds. The dead must slowly disappear.

He knows he cuts an odd figure amidst the sandstone ruins of century-old graves, stooping to read an epitaph or to pull out some weeds. His clothes are crumpled because he has neither the desire nor the energy to iron. Who is to see him other than the anonymous passengers on a passing silver train? He dresses up when Bert visits with his pink iced sponges and date scones, and they listen to music on Bert's old record player, songs from musicals and country and western, Bert singing along and tapping his feet against Ahmed's second-hand lounge. Bert sometimes asks him questions about his old life in Baghdad but Ahmed prefers his memories silent. When Bert goes home, Ahmed walks alone in the graveyard, practising his English on the gravestones. He says softly to himself, 'I was a professor in my old country. My son and my son-in-law died fighting our oppressors. I no longer believe in inherent goodness. I still pray though I no longer believe in God.'

As Ahmed returns to his house a silver train rushes past. He likes the noise the trains make, the way the tracks curve away from Central Station as though someone has taken particular care with their aesthetic. Sleekly silver, they disappear towards Redfern, blending with the grey stones sprinkled between the sleepers. Monotone: the soot-stained walls of the tunnels, the university tower, the terrace houses' slate roofs, the unforgiving gun metal of the roads.

The weather was perfect on his last trip into the city, the sky an opalescent blue; then during the night he heard a southerly wind come rattling in, the leaves of the neighbour's gum trees spiralling down, its twigs hitting the roof tiles, then rain, sheets and sheets of it slicing hard against the window. He likes the rain, its Australian intensity always surprising, just as he likes his trips west through Sydney's layers. Two cities – the wealthy one, with its million-dollar flats and shining department stores and botanical gardens and all the water, vast oceans of it. It laps at the stone harbour walls of Circular Quay and rustles after the green-and-yellow ferries, is neon-stained at night when people in their finery walk to the opera or sit under the stars drinking champagne and laughing loudly. But when the lines that divide all great cities are crossed, the roads develop potholes, the trees thin, leaving only bare streets and littered parks and tired amenities. In this part of Sydney many migrants have gathered, and the shops offer bread and rice and lentils and oil and dried fish from some faraway sea. Then the shops give way to dilapidated houses, to his house, the monumental masons and the business of burial.

Ahmed's gate is hanging on one hinge like a child's milk tooth held only by a filament of gum. The flyscreen on the front window seems to curl in greeting. He runs his hands

29

along a wall. 'Fibro', that was what Bert called it. What a flimsy house it is too, brittle and thin. It certainly wasn't built to last centuries, not like the houses in his old town where the walls spoke of birth and death through layers of whitewash and dust. A palm tree in his childhood's front garden dropped a dried frond from time to time onto rosebushes planted so long ago and so close together they formed a soft mélange of red and pink and yellow, each bush weaving into the other, the old limbs thick and thorny and bent.

The postman is walking slowly up the street, past the stone-masons' yards, past the blue house with the rotting veranda post and the vivisected car in the driveway. The postman's bag is light, not a trolley today, and he has stopped riding his little motorbike. Brown envelopes and a white one for those people, nothing for him. He'd watched the postman go into the cemetery one day to eat his lunch under a tree, sitting not on the gravestones but on the grass, looking at the graves as he ate, his head moving slowly left to right as he chewed, his postman's bag on the grass beside him. But no, the postman has turned back. A mistake. There is a letter now in Ahmed's rusty letterbox, not government brown: a flimsy crackling rice paper, one all the way from Indonesia. He waits until the postman is out of sight before walking down to the letterbox, taking the letter out, opening it. A letter in his daughter's hand, careful as she has been in every endeavour, each word measured, he knows, to allay his fears. He can no longer say the words 'wait', 'take small steps'.

They have travelled now for three months, on donkey carts and in the boots of cars, by bus and ship and aeroplane. She is closer, she writes.

The boatman is paid. My father. My dear, dear father. We will soon be with you again.

The flowering trees in the garden next door are bent low with damp flowers. Bees buzz around them, and the air seems mobile as Ahmed watches from his vantage point behind the venetian blinds. The wind makes snow of the petals and he takes a deep breath. It is honey he smells, lurid and thick. May the sea be smooth. May it be the perfect blue of a freshly planed lapis lazuli. May it be perfumed, as the air is all blossom now in this square, dry house. He knows his family will smell only salt and the fuel of the ship. But this is the olfactory surprise of it – as soon as land is near, perfumes will set out to meet their boat. May the little ones know this: land smells of clay and coffee and oil. Flowers, please; yes, flowers for the girls. And for his little grandson? The loamy promise of acres on which to grow tall and strong and proud of what is new and what he has left behind.

Before dinner, Ahmed walks again to the cemetery gates. The rain has made the paths treacherous – puddles, the ground slippery with ruts – but he is happy now his daughter and grandchildren are coming and there is so little time to wait. He finds a quiet grave in the sun and sits down carefully on the illegible name of its occupant. He closes his eyes and lets the sun turn his eyelids red and translucent, a far brighter red than the flowers in the Chinese cemetery, the red of his granddaughters' lips, the balloon he will buy at Paddy's Market for his grandson. There will be red flowers on the table when they make their first feast, vermilion pomegranates, blood-red cherries and wine-dark figs.

A shadow flits by him and he opens his eyes so quickly he is momentarily blinded by the sun's intensity. The postman has come back, he thinks.

'Good afternoon.'

He lifts his arm to shade his eyes. A young woman is walking alone, her hair as long and dark as his daughter's when he last saw her. 'Good afternoon.'

She is gone.

An hour later when it is again threatening rain he sees the girl kneeling before the rotting doors of a mausoleum, sketching the timber with the tips of her fingers. He watches for a moment from a distance. She is older than he thought. Her long hair gave her the look of a teenager but he suspects she is closer to his daughter's age, twenty-nine, almost thirty. Does she also have children? She seems too engrossed to notice the return of the rain, but he feels the drops and turns towards home. A drenching might lead to a cold, a cold to pneumonia: silly hypochondria, he knows, now his life has a waiting purpose. Soon he will take control of his family's new life.

By the time he is back in his house the rain is pelting down. He leaves the front door open so he can watch the rain forcing the overburdened branches of the flowering tree lower and lower, the flowers a sodden carpet beneath it. And there is the young woman running along the street, a cap on her head, an umbrella held high above it. She pauses for a moment as though deciding whether to seek shelter in the second stonemason's office. No, she has made a bolt for it and disappears down the street.

Now, Ahmed thinks, I am ready to eat – some bread, some olives and fruit. I will read my book and practise ways to speak English slowly, flatly, as the people speak when he walks up to Lidcombe, squinting at him, taking money from him delicately, as though his hands are dirty. He must stop thinking like this. He spends too much time alone, the television his only company. He watches the Special Broadcasting Service at night and if he's lucky he sees a film in a language he knows and each morning he watches the same news in many languages, the same footage, the same bombs.

As he closes the front door he looks back towards the cemetery gates. The sky has darkened, before too long the sun will set. I must pray, he thinks. Thanks for the living. Meditations for the dead. Prayers to take my mind from the images that descend with the night: sea monsters and pirates and giant waves and unscrupulous brokers and rusty, overcrowded little boats on a flaming sea. I am old, he thinks, and the old lose the elasticity of their optimism. Two new generations are coming and my life is good.

The Fret

Elizabeth lives on Beeni, a little island across the water
from Cura. You can walk to it at low tide across a causeway
rutted with seagrass. When the tide comes in the island's
inhabitants ring the bell that Tom, the island's unofficial
ferryman, has hung on a wooden frame for such a purpose.
At night the island looks towards Cura, brightly lit and
brash across the water. People who have cars leave them
over there. They park on Friday nights, their car headlights
sweeping across the water before being extinguished. They
pack their boxes of groceries into the prow of Tom's little
boat – bags of oranges, sacks of potatoes, the perishables that
have to be bought on the mainland and rowed across. The
island doesn't have a pub or a school, just a dozen houses
settled here and there around the perimeter like seabird nests.
Elizabeth writes during the day when everyone has gone
over to the mainland, when the island is silent save for dogs
barking or the shrill call of waterhens.

Elizabeth's house sits squat and misshapen above Lyle's Cove, the causeway to the right. Once it was a fisherman's hut. In the 1960s someone with money built a veranda across the front. Ten years later Elizabeth's uncle bought it and added a potter's studio at the back. It was here he created the bright and rotund pots that still dot the house. Elizabeth likes to sit on the veranda in one of her uncle's old wicker chairs to watch Tom row the island's children over to Cura. Later he takes the old women to the shops. At midday, when the tide is out, she might see a solitary walker picking their way across the exposed causeway. Late in the day the sun slants in, the water rises and Tom begins again, backwards and forwards, ferrying people home until it's dark; the sharp pull on the bell, the hollow slap of the oars as Tom and his passenger slide homewards across the bay.

Not many people come to visit her – her brother, Dan, but rarely. A year ago Ed Walker, a fellow poet, spent a few weeks here. As she watched him walk across the causeway Elizabeth knew that whatever their friendship had been before, they'd sleep together during his stay. He walked across the water, his straw hat on the back of his head, a rucksack slung over his left shoulder.

'I'm glad you could come.'

'Hello, Elizabeth.' He kissed her.

She led him to the studio and watched him unpack. She knew what she'd done. 'You don't invite a man to your room if you don't intend to sleep with him,' her mother had cautioned before Elizabeth went away to university. Of course her mother was right.

It didn't happen straight away. She and Ed spent ten days wandering the island, Lyle's Cove and Water Hen Bay with its reeds and oyster leases and stalking crabs, the flat, marshy grasslands in the middle of the island. They worked in the afternoon in their respective writing spaces, Ed in the studio tapping away at Uncle's old typewriter, even though he'd brought a laptop with him, Elizabeth in the little closed-in room at the end of the veranda, the flywire walls singing as the breeze caught them. In the evening they sat on the veranda with a glass of wine and watched Tom row to and from Cura. They recited the poetry they loved.

They went over to Cura a couple of times during Ed's stay, Ed to check his email and to see the pub, Elizabeth to shop and pick up any letters from her brother. They sat in the smoky bar under the blackened and useless lobster pots some enterprising publican had hoisted to the ceiling years before for character. They listened as the old men talked about what fish were running, and looked at their raw, brown faces. Ed got so excited about the yellowtail runs that he talked Tom into lending them one of his boats and they rowed until they saw the water flicker with the shoal. They didn't fish, just sat and watched the water undulate and shiver and talked about poetry and what it meant to them.

Over the two weeks of Ed's stay the tension slowly built till it reminded Elizabeth of storm clouds rolling up from the south, the kind of storm that is heralded by a sharp drop in temperature, the trees urgently whispering like a group of gossips, the birds flying with their heads down. Tension building up: you have to sleep together just to let it out. She'd watched Ed for days, the black chest hairs visible above the top button of his shirt, the way he flicked his thick hair off his face, or twisted his wineglass thoughtfully as he talked about John Donne or Walt Whitman. The air bristled whenever he came into the kitchen and stood behind her. He asked what she thought of Robert Bridges, Elizabeth Bishop, Judith Wright. She asked him why he was asking. She liked all kinds of poetry so surely her favourites were irrelevant. The clouds appeared then faded above Cura. The rain came and went. The sunset slanted across the sea, turning it red. Elizabeth lit a candle and watched it flicker beside her wineglass.

On Ed's last Friday night Tom rowed them back from the pub in Cura. They walked along the beach to the house. Their feet made sucking noises in the sand. Ed pulled her towards him just as they reached the veranda and drew her down onto the grass. It's happened at last, she thought. Their cries might have been mistaken for birdcall, for the surprising and cruel brush of sea against rock. Their shadows danced with the shadows of the night. The bell rang out and Tom rowed to and from Cura. The next morning they ate breakfast as though nothing had happened.

'I'll go back at midday tomorrow,' Ed said. 'I have to collect my son at Minna Minna.'

Elizabeth hasn't had many visitors since then. The winter was cold and wet, the spring not much better. One powerfully windy night a house in Cura lost its roof. The fishing boats were beached for weeks at a time. Elizabeth walked around the island enjoying the stinging rain on her face. No one dared to use the causeway so Tom was kept busy. Even when the tide was low the water ran treacherous with rips that snatched at your ankles and tried to pull you down.

She was sick of the weather by the time the summer came around again.

Her brother wrote to say he was coming to see her. By then the summer weather had descended, a thick, damp blanket. Before Beeni, when she'd lived for a while down the south coast, she'd spend weekends in Sydney with her friends then drive back down to the little community in which she taught, back to her school and her students, too many of them already aware of life's limitations. A long, wet summer had turned the coast tropical. The tender backyard banana trees, their fringed leaves sadly swaying, the cockatoos hanging upside down from power lines, all of it made her homesick for something she'd never quite had. Not something she'd talk to friends about, this feeling. Dan was like one of those acrobatic cockatoos. In and out of hospital, his moods up, then down, the drugs making his skin dry and crusty, especially around his eyes. He looked like someone befuddled by a long, deep sleep. Then he'd disappear again and the worry would start. He'd send postcards from far away: the Pilbara, Townsville, fishing off Albany, shearing in western New South Wales. In some he wrote in an elegant, measured voice, in others he was florid. He'd come back to Elizabeth eventually, too skinny, his jeans loose around bony hips.

Tom brought him over on the morning tide. Dan was far thinner and more brashly outspoken than Elizabeth remembered.

'How's the writing going, Lizzie?' he asked.

'Slowly. It takes a long time to germinate a poem.' She laughed. 'Desperation is not good for poetry, that's why I moved here.'

She let him settle in, thinking he'd want some private space but he was keen to talk. He told her about some books he'd just read, a film that had moved him, his favourite music. She talked about her thesis. The trips out to the university, her train announcing itself with a puff of cold air as it rushed into Wynyard station. Her thesis was an examination of the early colony's burial practices, based on a study of cemeteries from Rookwood to Windsor. She'd clambered through blackberry in search of hidden mounds. Peered into a family vault in Sackville. In Ebeneezer she'd found a whole colony of children belonging to one family, every child dead before they reached their first year. Roland and Oliver, Estella and Charles and Enoch and Abel and Emma, names straight out of Dickens, their fates just as cruel as in one of his plots.

'So, what's next?' she asked as they circled the island, just as she and Ed had done, picking their way over rock pools, daring the still-dangerous tide. Dan told her about ending it with a woman he'd loved. About going down to Young, to the meatworks where refugees were being hired because there was a labour shortage. 'But you're not a refugee, Dan,' she said and he looked at her oddly and answered, 'Yeah, I know, but I've seen terrible things in my head.'

She told him about her night with Ed the previous summer. How she couldn't be bothered with lovers anymore.

'You always stayed too remote, Lizzie,' Dan said. 'I couldn't be like you. I reckon that's what sent me over the edge. You've got to be around people. Talk to people, lead a sociable life.' He threw a piece of driftwood to a dog, bending so low Elizabeth saw the knobs of his spine and the vulnerable child he'd remained. He said, 'I want to put my life together again, Lizzie. Find someone nice. Settle down.'

'You have a home here.' She looked across at Cura, at a sea fret stretching across the tops of the hills, hanging there, a long white finger of cloud, as fragile as Dan's spine and the life ahead of him.

On his last night they sat in the old wicker chairs and talked about Elizabeth's research. Her doctorate was nearly finished. 'Why don't you stay here?' she asked again.

Dan rolled a cigarette. 'Oh, Lizzie. This place is as dead as those cemeteries you visit. It would send me even madder.'

The tide was out the next morning so Dan didn't need Tom to row him across, but Tom stood beside Elizabeth and smoked a thoughtful cigarette as they watched Dan go. The water winked and shuddered its own kind of anguish. Dan might as well have been walking on a poem, Elizabeth thought, or a chimera of one, all sliding words and rhythms and stanzas. He turned halfway across the causeway and raised his hand above his head. Elizabeth waved back.

'He's a character, that brother of yours,' Tom said, squinting across at Cura. 'He'll just make it. Another ten minutes and the tide will turn.'

Elizabeth walks the island, looking into the closed week-enders, seeing their not-quite-right furniture, cast off, relocated: old tables and chairs, recycled lounges, make-do things for carefree places. Postcards arrive from Dan, one from Young, one from New England, another from a country town up the coast. He talks of new friends, Aboriginal stockmen or the men he met at Central Station, looking for work and prepared to go anywhere. *New Australians, seekers of asylum*, new people who make do like weekender furniture, not quite of its place.

She sits on the wide veranda and drinks a glass of wine. Her poems arrive in moments like this, each one a suggestion at first, a shadow, a hint. They take her to better places when she's ready for bed. The bell rings. Tom rows across to Cura like a water-bug trailing in a wake. And deep in the night under the mosquito net, she hears the impatient call of a poem, and rows to it and guides it home.

Dein ist Mein Ganzes Herz

Bert Hamilton loved *Oklahoma*. He started the car and pushed a CD into the player: 'The Surrey with the Fringe on Top'. He sang along as he turned onto Lawrence Hargrave Drive. No chicks or ducks or geese in sight, just a few surfers offshore waiting for a wave, the sea a milky green, soft, like old memories. He was glad he'd taken after his father. His dad had loved singing too, especially in the bathroom. His favourite song was Franz Lehar's 'You Are My Heart's Delight', *Dein ist mein ganzes herz*, if you wanted to be German about it. He'd relished the song's tender nuances as he washed away the metallic scents of a shift at the steelworks, a romantic singing a love song while Bert's mother darned in the kitchen. A no-nonsense wife. Sing all you like, she seemed to say, her needle stabbing. Just leave me the darning and cooking and putting the kids to bed.

Bert drove slowly past Coledale Public School, careful to stay within the speed limit. Coledale Beach was deserted too, the rain of the past few days deterring people, he supposed, though today's sky was blue enough. Out on the horizon half a dozen tankers awaited the go-ahead to enter Port Kembla Harbour. Some parrots screeched from the branches of a Norfolk pine. He'd allowed two hours to get up to Sydney. More than enough time, barring something unforeseen. You could never predict it, though. He'd been stuck behind a funeral cortege the last time he drove up, on the Heathcote Road making for Woronora Cemetery. He never overtook funeral cars though most people ignored that old etiquette. No hats to take off, no crossing yourself or saying 'white horse, black horse' to scare away bad luck. Things had changed a lot since he was a boy.

The sea-bridge now, not another car on it. He drove slowly, admiring the pale ocean on one side, the flaking cliffs on the other, then the Coalcliff mine, the climb up to Bald Hill, the gauzy grey-green of the bush beside the freeway slowly giving way to the suburbs of Sutherland Shire, the least interesting part of Sydney, he'd decided, a view formed after he'd discovered Villawood.

'Oh, what a beautiful morning.' He wished Sandy was still alive. She'd be singing along with him now. Well, it certainly was a beautiful morning, the air fresh and salty even though he'd left the sea behind. Singing along to *Oklahoma*, *South Pacific*, *The Sound of Music*. She'd certainly loved *that* one. Went to see it half-a-dozen times, the film and the live production. 'You should join a choir, love,' he'd said many times but she'd not been keen. Said her voice wasn't good enough. It was, though, clear and strong.

'You are my heart's delight', words passed from father to son through a bathroom's closed door. Bert had sung it to Sandy when they were courting. Sandy wasn't like his mother at all. She understood love songs. She sang along with Bert for the rest of her life – to Lehar songs, to songs from all their favourite musicals. Happy. Singing always made them happy. It was really something when he and Sandy moved into their own house in Austinmer, away from the smoke and noise of the steelworks, lying in bed and listening to the sea, to the goods trains shaking the whole house with the weight of their loads of coal or pig iron. Like his father, he'd worked at the steelworks for thirty years and when he turned sixty he and Sandy talked a lot about what they'd do when Bert retired. More time for shows in Sydney; they might even go over to London and see some shows there. *Cats. Les Misérables. The Phantom of the Opera.* Not the same as the old ones, though. *Showboat, The King and I, Kismet.* Then Sandy got sick and died.

How could anyone ever explain how sad they felt when the love of their life passed away before them? No point in trying. He just went on – to the bowling club for dinner, a flutter on the pokies, a couple of beers. He walked on the beach a lot, spent more and more time in the garden with his tomatoes. Listened for hours on end to his records. Didn't sing much, just listened and thought a lot about how tricky life was. It took a few years to pull himself together. He retired. Did some voluntary work for the South Coast Labour Council. Heard his mother's voice telling him to stop mooning – *Busy hands. The Lord helps them who help themselves* – but he also heard his father's tenor, richer with the acoustic enhancement of the bathroom tiles. *My Heart's Delight.* Well, Sandy was and she always would be his. So he started to sing again, in the kitchen, in the bathroom, just like his dad.

Bert turned at King George's Road and headed west. He had to be at Villawood by two. As he drove he looked at the houses, the frangipani trees covered in white and yellow flowers, the neat brick verandas and fences, the shops. He and Sandy had always enjoyed a trip up to the city. Sometimes they caught the train because the parking was too expensive, but most of the time they drove up and took their chances on the city streets, braving the lumbering buses and arrogant drivers and pedestrians who seemed hell-bent on getting themselves run over. He often wished Sandy had come to Villawood with him. The things they'd have talked about if she had. What would she have made of the shops in Granville? The different foods and spices and all the different smells? And talk about singing. Some of the songs he'd heard on the shops' record-players defied description. They were more than songs, more like a long, slow keening. Lebanese mostly, well, from somewhere in the Middle East. He was slowly learning the differences between the countries and where they were. Funny how a place could be familiar because you heard it mentioned on the news but you never really knew where it was. Beside the sea. Landlocked. Three-quarters desert. Mountainous. Flat. They all spoke the same language, he'd thought, until someone put him straight. Some weren't even Arabs. Better get your info right, Bert, he'd said to himself and he'd gone to Dymocks to get an atlas and after that he'd sat with it in his lap as he watched the evening news and traced each country as it was mentioned.

He had to buy some cakes today, some magazines, a pot plant, he'd decided, last time he'd visited. People liked to have something to look after and they weren't allowed pets in there. Today he'd buy his cakes in Strathfield at Irina's Cake Shop in Redmyre Road. He'd happened on Irina's a few months back. Coming home, the highway a mess of closed lanes and cranky drivers, he'd nipped across to Strathfield thinking he'd be better off on The Boulevard, but the traffic that side was just as bad and when he saw the cake shop he decided he might as well pick up something for tea, a steak and kidney pie or a Cornish pastie; he'd get half-a-dozen and freeze the spares for later. He was impressed by the blue-and-white curtains in the window, the way Irina had organised a three-tiered cake display and, to the left of it, a lovely silver samovar. When he asked her about it she told him she'd bought it in Sydney and they'd laughed at the irony. Travel halfway round the world to buy something from home. 'I'm Bert,' he'd said, extending his hand, and she'd returned hers, so white, so cool, and said, 'Irina.' He'd been back to the cake shop quite a few times since, ordering coffee, eating a cake or two.

On his last visit Irina had been leaning against the counter deep in thought. She didn't recognise him at first and then she surfaced like a diver coming up from the deep. 'Bert,' she said, her accent making it 'Bet'.

'How are you, Irina?' He knew he was saying her name wrong too. *Eye*rina when it should have been *Ear*ina. Different backgrounds, different parts of the face.

She smiled when he ordered a coffee and a couple of almond shortbreads. Then he looked across to the pie warmer and asked her to box him a couple of pies and a couple of sausage rolls.

'You don't want now?'

'Tonight,' he said. 'That's my tea.' Then, 'Well, not all of it. I'm not that much of a pig.' He sat, glanced at the local paper spread on the tabletop.

She passed his coffee, went back to leaning on the counter.

'Why don't you have a coffee too? My shout,' said Bert.

Irina went over to the coffee machine and frothed some milk. Seeing he'd demolished the shortbreads, she put a couple more on a plate.

'You work near here?' Her voice was barely audible above the coffee machine.

'Work? No, love, I'm retired. Just passing through. I live down the coast. And what about you? How long have you had this place?'

She sat across from him and raised her coffee to her lips delicately. 'Five years.'

'Five years, eh? That how long you've been here?'

'In Strathfield? In Australia?'

'In Australia.'

'Twenty years.'

'Always had cake shops?'

She looked at him oddly. Laughed. 'No. I work in factory in Chippendale. Terrible.'

'You've done well to get your own place.'

She said nothing to that. 'You have kids, Bert?'

'No. What about you?'

'No.'

In the silence they both looked towards the street where the traffic flowed, stopped, moved on slowly, an oddly choreographed performance from which petrol fumes danced into the shop.

'Well, there you go,' he said.

'I was left money by friend in Russia. I like to cook. I bought shop.'

'Left money, eh? That's lucky. No one in my family had any money to leave.'

'Not relative.'

'Friend, you said?'

'Not real friend.'

'Workmate?'

'Not work.'

Bert bit into his third shortbread. He'd be the size of a bus if he didn't have a good metabolism. He'd go for a walk when he got home. He was spending too much time sitting now that he was driving up and down to Sydney so often.

'This man was good to me in Russia. I did things for him.'

Bert took in the tightness around Irina's mouth, her eyes suddenly hooded, as though she was looking inwards, to deeper memories. He'd seen that look often enough. Since becoming a visitor to Villawood he'd met people who'd experienced things he couldn't even imagine. His mother was often saying, *There's always someone worse off than you.* Well, she'd certainly been right about that. A house in Bexley, then Wollongong, and Austi. Father, mother, brothers. Nothing dramatic, nothing dangerous. Sandy going was the worst thing that had happened to him and he hoped he never had to go through grief like that again.

Irina's face was pale, unlined. Her eyes were blue like his but more the colour of cornflowers or the kind of sky you'd see over Austinmer Beach on a hot summer's day, a deep blue that held within it kids' laughter and beach umbrellas and seagulls and the scents of an Aussie summer, the sea, suntan lotion, hot chips from the takeaway opposite the beach. Irina returned his scrutiny just as intently. What did she see, he wondered. Just a bloke on the cusp of seventy, skinny, balding, beach skin brown and tough and dry.

'I lived in little village.' She sighed. 'Too small for you to care about name. Five house. One cow. Half-a-dozen chickens. You know this little small places? You know very, very small town? My father worked on railways. Put gravel between tracks. Each day he spread it, each night he come home. Winter so cold the shovel froze to his skin through his glove. Quiet. Nothing there. I left for Moscow as soon as I was fifteen. Not right in city. Suburbs. I wanted to go to school but cleaned. Hotel rooms. Big hotels. For Westerners.'

Bert nodded. Working class he knew well enough but not poor like the people he met in Villawood. Poor, frightened people who relied on food drops and refugee camps, who watched their kids turn to skeletons and endured this because there was no alternative. People over whom destiny seemed to have passed a cold, indifferent hand.

'You know about Russia?'

'Not a lot, love.'

'Moscow was poor. Too many changes. Lonely. I got trolley bus to work, then metro. Metro was warm. Very nice. Lots of people. Everyone hurry, hurry, hurry. Cleaning hotel eight till lunch. Back at five. That was for cleaning up people who rented room for day. Party officials. Westerners who had to catch aeroplane to another place. People who had enough money to pay for girls then go home to wife.'

She indicated his empty cup but Bert shook his head. He'd be wanting to pee all the way home if he drank any more. Some schoolkids came in and Irina got up to serve them. She returned when they'd gone and started again, dreamily.

'I liked to clean. Big rooms. Hot water. Bath. Radio. Little cakes of soap. Russian girls now go to West for sex. They go away in bus, in car. Once we left because of Communism, now they leave to be models. Which is worse? To be poor, to be brainwashed? Best take whichever feeds you.'

Bert looked around the shop. The lino was spotless, the tops of the little tables all clean and free from crumbs. She'd put a vase with a silk rose on each table and through the curtains, so blue and white and crisp, he could make out the rotund shape of the samovar, polished, silver and gleaming.

'I was asked by man to be his friend. Special friend.'

'I think I get the gist of it,' Bert said.

She stood. 'That is why I have shop.'

What could he say? I understand. It doesn't matter as long as you keep your dignity. As long as you are kind to other people and forgive them their sins as you forgive your own. He stood too. 'I'd better get going.' He picked up his pies and sausage rolls and walked towards the door, turned back and waved, and Irina waved too.

Bert turned the car towards Strathfield. He was hungry. He stopped at the cake shop every time he was up now. It wasn't just that he liked seeing Irina or eating her cakes or chatting about life as he ate a pie or some shortbread or one of her little fig pastries fragrant with unfamiliar spices. When he was in the cake shop he felt as though some new vista had opened to him, snow-soft as a Moscow winter, as white as a new page on which you might rewrite your life. He'd go to Granville after Irina's; there were cakes and cakes, after all, and he knew what his Villawood friends liked: baklava and halva and fruit – mangoes especially, and bananas for the little kids, though the price of bananas these days…but never mind about that. He went back to Irina's because when someone tells you something special about their life the least you can do is let them know you aren't shocked, even if you are. That life is strange and the best anyone can offer is the gift of understanding, even if you don't understand at all.

He parked out the front and was surprised as he walked in to see not Irina at the counter but an old woman who was busy serving some men in overalls. The men were loudly ordering, a dozen pies, a dozen cakes, morning tea for their workmates, Bert presumed, and he felt a little stab of loss for all the days he'd spent in overalls, eating Sandy's packed lunches in the work canteen and talking about football or the goings-on of various politicians.

Their food packed neatly in a cardboard box, the men paid and left and Bert stood at the counter wondering what to eat and where Irina was.

'Can I help?'

'How are you?' said Bert. 'Nice day.'

When the old woman nodded he saw the resemblance, a face much older but with the same scaffolding, the same cheekbones and blue eyes.

'You Irina's mum?'

The woman looked at him curiously. 'I am aunt. And you are Bet?'

Bert felt a cold chill move down his spine. Well, how about that. 'Yeah, I am. Is Irina okay?'

'Have to go to city. Back later.'

He looked out towards the now-familiar street, the tubs of flowers caked in car fumes and dust, a dog tethered to a pole and waiting in the way loyal dogs wait, its look intense and hopeful each time a new person passed. In the cake-fragrant shop he saw himself in that patient dog. The thought did not trouble him. There were worse creatures to compare yourself to.

'Okay,' he said. 'I'd better order and get on my way.'

He scrutinised the cakes in the glass-topped counter, walked over to the window and peered through the curtains at the three-tiered display, settling on a couple of cream-filled sponges, their pink icing glossy and hard. The little kids would like these; kids always liked sweet pink things, didn't they? Shy, they'd stand behind their parents and reach out for the freshly cut slices, smile at him, the deadness he'd seen in their eyes banished, if just for a moment, by the cake's promise of jam and sugar and cream.

He paid and as Irina's aunt passed his change back he said, 'Give Irina my best wishes,' making sure he got the pronunciation right, because you should respect a person's proper name.

Later that day, the drive back along the coast more thoughtful, more pregnant with all he'd seen and heard, he was welcomed by the gauzy bush, by the drifts of coreopsis beside the freeway, yellow as gobs of egg yolk. He looked at the sea and thought about all the ships that had come to this coast. What must it have looked like to people who'd lived in Britain's teeming streets or jails? The great slab of the escarpment sliced with landslides and erosion, the grand trees from whose branches birds squawked. What a paradise it must have seemed. It still did. The slow drive down the first treacherous bends of Stanwell Tops, the descent into the beauty of the beaches, always lifted his spirits as insistently as any favourite song.

When he got home he walked around the house. Every house has a feel to it, he knew, a welcoming scent, a moment of embrace when all the cares of the day disappear into the familiar. My place. My home. He felt too keenly, perhaps, for Sandy, who should have been here too. But she still was in some way. He let his eyes play across the laminated kitchen table, the salt and pepper shakers and the sauce bottle awaiting his pies, the canisters that had been a wedding present. He looked out through the window to the garden beyond, where Sandy had been standing so many times when he'd arrived home, the newly washed clothes in the basket, the pegs in the plastic container that hung from the clothes line. He sang as he prepared his dinner, familiar songs of love and loss learned down the years: a genetics of song. And later, when night fell, he stood in the garden under the trembling stars and looked for the Southern Cross.

The Remote Lands of Art

The translator sat back in his chair and looked at the poet's name. In red ink he wrote his own name, *Masaki Tanaka*, underneath, then *translator*. He had been translating the work of the poet for the past ten years. Readers in Japan were awaiting this next collection, *The Remote Lands of Art*, the title taken from Schiller. Next he wrote the title in Japanese then neatly repositioned the manuscript on his desk. The poet lived in the remote and dry Australian countryside yet his words always seemed to speak to his readers in a lush voice. After a recent trip to Sydney, where he'd been the guest translator at a writers' festival, Masaki had made a side trip to visit the poet at his house. The countryside around it was a sea of dancing wheat, and Masaki and the poet had sat drinking beer from short bottles on the poet's veranda, the glass densely perspiring in the afternoon heat. They'd looked across the landscape to a newly ploughed field, the soil red, a low cloud of dirt rising from it like a heat haze. Despite his prolific output, the poet was a man of few spoken words.

They'd sat on in the companionable silence for ten, twenty minutes, the air around them brittle and dry. On the table the beer bottles left small damp circles that soon disappeared in the heat.

The poet said to Masaki, 'How do you say "rainbow" in Japanese?' and Masaki replied *niji*.

The poet contemplated the answer and in the silence Masaki heard something that sounded like a woman sighing. It was the grass seeds rattling against the house and the field of ripe dry wheat stems seemed to echo a response.

'Not many rainbows out here. You need rain for a rainbow, or at least the threat of it,' the poet said.

In his mind Masaki repeated 'threat of rain': *ama moyō*. He preferred the sound of the words in English. There was something thuggish about them, as though rain clouds were advancing with truncheons or guns. English expressions had delighted him from the very first time he'd sat through a cowboy film as a child, John Wayne looming from the screen, his dubbed voice sometimes asserting itself from behind the Japanese. Words with short, blunt force like *Texas* and *steer* and *gun* and *rancher*. He'd often thought this was why he'd been attracted to Australian writing, because, like Texas, Australia spoke of the wide open and the rough and isolated.

When the poet moved in his chair Masaki prepared to rise. He put his half-empty beer bottle on the table and uncrossed his knees, but the poet just leaned forwards, squinting into the sky. 'Is that a bird?' he said.

Masaki peered too. 'Yes, I think it is, but it's a long way away.'

'Probably a wedge-tailed eagle; I heard some of the farmers talking about them the other day. They hate them, you know. Reckon they take the lambs.' He put his hand to his eyes. 'I can't see it now.'

Masaki could still make out a tiny black mark, a pin pricking the radiant blue. He didn't say this to the poet.

'Now,' the poet said. 'What more do you need me to do?'

'Nothing,' Masaki said. 'What we've discussed this afternoon clarifies everything. I'll make the changes you suggested. I'll email a copy of the manuscript before it goes to Tokyo.'

'Thanks. It's all lost on me, of course.'

'At least you'll have the file.'

They stood, Masaki politely taking the beer bottles through to the kitchen. He thought he should tip the remainder of his beer down the sink but the poet said, 'Leave it, I'll finish it later.'

Masaki took a last look around the poet's lounge room, so dark and shadowy after the scorched brightness of outside. The floorboards were covered in old rugs, the couch draped with brightly coloured crocheted blankets. On the walls were works by many famous Australian artists. The poet had introduced Masaki to them when he'd arrived. He'd told him about his friendship with Lloyd Rees, the artist's paintings becoming more impressionistic and abstract as he slowly lost his sight. 'But he was Australia's Turner, don't you think?'

Masaki said yes, the yellows and ochres of the Lloyd Rees in question looked a lot like one of Turner's paintings of the Thames.

'Okay,' the poet said as they walked down the front steps to Masaki's hire car. They shook hands. 'Thanks. It can't be easy turning some of those Aussie expressions into Japanese ones.'

Masaki smiled. 'No, not always, but your poetry is so interesting the challenge is in capturing the spirit of it, not just the words.'

A tractor was moving slowly across the horizon, pulling a thick cloud of dust behind it. Its plough raised, it looked like a scorpion about to strike, Masaki thought. The poet was watching the tractor's progress closely too and Masaki wondered what imagery it suggested to him and whether it might find its way into a poem.

The poet said slowly, 'Is your family okay?'

'Excuse me?'

'Your family in Japan, are they affected by this Fukushima business?'

'No. Like me, they live a long way from there.'

'Good to hear. Dreadful, just dreadful.'

Masaki didn't need to ask the poet such questions. He already knew about him from fan sites, the internet, from book biographies topped with publicity photos that made the poet look newly washed and gormless and not like himself at all. Never married, lived with his mother. But who was the person to whom he dedicated poems of enduring love? Like Shakespeare's dark lady, a mysterious person for whom the poet poured forth his poems.

The hire car's windscreen was covered in a thin layer of red dust. Masaki squirted water onto it and turned the wipers on, transforming it into red mud. The poet smiled and Masaki ran the water and wipers again until the mess cleared.

'Left then right through the town. The highway is two kilometres on. Okay?'

Masaki nodded. Once out of sight he'd turn on the car's global positioning but he wanted the poet to think he knew his way around the country as efficiently as he moved through his poems, familiar with the landmarks, the dips and rises, the signs.

As he drove away he watched the poet in his rear-vision mirror slowly ascend the house's front steps and go through the front door. The poet had lived out here with his mother until she died a few years ago. He was sixty-eight now, healthy. He might live like this for another thirty years, all of which promised many more years of translating. Masaki found this very satisfying and thoughts of the poet accompanied him through the lonely countryside until he reached the bigger towns, then the suburbs and Sydney.

Masaki glanced out his window. In a pot on his balcony he'd planted a dwarf cherry tree and it was preparing to flower. Pink buds had lined up along its branches. They looked like knotted silk scarves about to be snatched by the wind. In a week the flowers would burst open. He'd always wanted to be present at that moment, but the cherry flowers always opened on their own and in secret. In a week he would sit at his desk, distracted by the silky gradations of pink and white, the yellow starburst of the stamens. He would remember his childhood visits to see the arcades of cherry trees in blossom, his family picnicking under the trees' flower-laden branches, the petals drifting down.

What would the poet make of that?

Masaki went into his small lounge room, its spare furnishings monotone. He had always liked things in their place. Perhaps that was why he'd become a translator, putting words in their proper order, mastering something foreign. His childhood prairies, those John Wayne words taking shape in his mouth as though he were sucking a stone. Then afterwards, university and his first translating assignments: journalism, business reports and finally, happily, poetry. He had made the transition because he was a poet himself back then, though he'd given up writing his own poetry a long time ago. He had made his name as a translator when he'd helped some American poets in Japan on a visiting writers' scheme; he'd worked on one of their chapbooks which sold well in the USA. Lance Everton, that was the American poet's name, a very tall man from Texas whose voice had a nasal twang not unlike a movie star cowboy's. He'd even walked in the bow-legged way of John Wayne, as though he'd ridden horses all his life. 'Lance Everton.' He said the name out loud and as he did so, the words of one of Lance's poems came to him, a love poem written to an old girlfriend who lived in Fort Worth.

Sometimes Bird song
Travels faster than Sound
Might overtake bombs
Might even Overtake love.

Like a lot of poets, Lance Everton had died young.

Masaki made a little pot of green tea, the kind with brown rice grains through it. It always made him think of Marcel Proust and his lime-flower tea and Madeleine cake. For the Japanese such a nostalgic memory would be a pot of brown-rice green tea or the urgent pink scent of cherry blossoms on a warm spring day.

And for him there was also Kasumi, of course.

He'd known his memories would eventually lead to her: he always remembered Kasumi when he thought about cherry blossoms. He had first seen her at a foreign writers' conference in Nagasaki, her English interpreter in the chair next to her. Kasumi sat perfectly still, long hair draped over her left shoulder, eyes down, concentrating on the interpreter's words. Masaki had stood in the doorway, watching. Kasumi's concentration was the immobility of an ancient statue, marble lines, hands clasped – she might have been praying – the interpreter whispering the words into her ear. English words into Japanese, Kasumi frozen by them.

Masaki called the poet at six. He had read the manuscript again before going out with friends for lunch and when he'd come home he felt the pull of one of the poet's phrases, a comic piece in which the poet had called a friend 'a jesting ludicrous dag'. Masaki leafed through the manuscript and when he reached 'Poem to Joe', he read those words out loud. He knew what they meant and how they might be used playfully, but the poem referred to a lost friend of the poet's, someone he had cared for and with whom he'd lost touch. As in much of his work, the poet used the metaphors of the bush, the dirt, the slap of dry winds, the infinite and indifferent skies and half-dead crops representing people, reconstructing them as part of the landscape. For the poet the Australian bush seemed a place onto which God had both smiled and frowned. To him it seemed a wayward land full of wayward people:

> You were an old mate, Dust brother
> Crop-dusted lord of this busted kingdom, Dust brother
> A jesting ludicrous dag.

Masaki wanted to ask the poet if the poem should carry the same emotional resonance of a poem like Kenneth Slessor's 'Five Bells', that great Australian love poem to a lost friend.

The poet's phone rang on and on and Masaki heard it in the old wooden house, the crocheted rugs hot and prickling in the evening heat, the blind artist's yellow painting like sunlight above them. He tried to call the poet for a few days after that. The page proofs had come back from Tokyo and *The Remote Lands of Art* just needed Masaki's sign-off to go to the printer. 'Poem to Joe' still bothered him, though. He needed to talk to the poet again about his intent.

Masaki looked out at the cherry tree. The blossoms were a little more open today, as was his memory of Kasumi. He had married her six months after first seeing her. He knew he was as much in love with her immobility and her fixed concentration on the interpreter's words as he was with her. He saw that stillness in her often. He might read to her, he might translate some English into Japanese or tell her the latest news of the famous Australian poet whose poetry was so popular in Japan because it spoke of friendship and love in different ways. The poems caused people to sit still and listen intensely to the poet's odd allegories and metaphors, the locating of the riches of love in a poor, dry place. Kasumi carried that kind of stillness in everything she did. It was almost mythological – a goddess might possess it – but it was deadly too, like the stillness of a corpse, all life gone from it. Masaki had seen dead eyes in a dead face. He knew how a

dead face became a Noh mask, nothing to animate it once
the soul had retreated.

And just as life leaked away, so too did love. In one of
his poems the poet had spoken of love as a colander. Masaki
had sought the best Japanese word, deciding on *korandā*,
because it was so close to the English. The poet had spoken
of love draining away as though the human body were
pricked all over with little holes. He had written of a human
vessel from which love seeped: the heart certainly, and from
the eyes as tears and also the fingertips, touch no longer firm
and confident but bloodless. Love dripped from the body
slowly before you realised it was gone. Masaki had written
a poem to Kasumi about dying love but he'd never showed
it to her.

'You married?' the poet had asked during Masaki's visit.

'Divorced.'

Kasumi, still as a lotus flower, came to him sometimes in
the night, often in the scratch of his pen when writing on
a computer just wouldn't do. Eyes down, hands clasped, her
features chalk. Dead love turns the body into a desert. Once
love has drained away the body dries and dies. He saw the
wedge-tailed eagle in the blue distance, the poet's eyes not
seeing what Masaki's could. When Kasumi had left he'd
written a poem to her. He was proud of it, though he knew
the words, the rhythms and rhymes, were influenced as
much by the Australian poet's as by his own ideas.

He called the poet again that evening. Finally, a woman
answered. 'Mr Masaki?' she repeated when he said who he

was. 'Haven't you heard? He died a couple of days ago. He had a cerebral haemorrhage.'

'No. I hadn't heard,' Masaki said, his voice bones. 'In hospital?'

'Oh no. He was sitting on his front veranda when he went.'

As she talked Masaki saw Kasumi again, her statue-self, as an English poem was whispered into her ears in Japanese.

He thanked the poet's friend. He dialled his publisher in Tokyo to tell him the news. It was too late now to change anything. He looked out at the unfurling cherry tree, seeing in its emerging pinks and whites the hard ochre and blue of the poet's rainbow land, and the threatening clouds with their truncheons and guns moving stealthily across it.

He said to the publisher, 'I also have found a new poem which I'd like to include in the collection. The poet sent it to me just before he died. I'll email it to you now so you can add it to the manuscript.' And as he spoke he scratched out the words *'To Kasumi' by Masaki Tanaka*, and wrote instead *'To a Love, Lost' by Les Cartwright*.

The Rabbit

The boy turns the pages of the book, his fingers carefully tracing the words as he reads. *It is a sunny day and Jim and Annie are going to a farm.* He looks carefully at Jim in his neat blue shirt. Annie is wearing a red-and-white dress. She has golden hair like her brother and very blue eyes. They smile on each page, waking in beds covered with striped blankets, going to school in an orange bus, eating pink ice-creams with their friends. The farm has a cow and a field with an apple tree. Some chickens peck at the ground. Jim will milk the cow and Annie will collect the eggs, the boy reads. There is one brown egg and six are white.

The teacher gives the class a different book each week, old books, their blue covers written on already by other children. The boy finds something companionable in the previous readers' words and little sketches, as though they are pointing out things that he might miss. In one book Jim and Annie have been to the zoo, in others to the circus and to a supermarket to buy food. They have visited a friend in hospital and Jim has decided he'll become a doctor when he grows up. They have gone on holidays to a faraway mountain and learned how to ski on its snowy slopes.

The boy likes best the books with animals in them. The black-and-white cow gazes at him over a white-painted fence. The chickens peck at bright green grass. A yellow bird sits in the branches of the apple tree, its head thrown back, musical notes rising from its open mouth. When Jim goes with the farmer to milk the cow a little dog goes with them. Jim and Annie have many opportunities to play with animals. The boy hopes for such times one day.

The boy's mother sits in the corner and listens to him read. Sometimes she repeats the words after him.

Let's buy some oranges today, Jim. Watch me ski, Annie.

Sometimes the boy prefers to read silently; it helps him store the words in his head, to imagine the world of Jim and Annie better, the lives that go on after the story has ended, when the hens are back on their perches and the cow is milked. The dog and the farmer will sleep after helping Jim to milk the cow. The boy has even made up his own Jim and Annie stories, placing them both in parks and schoolrooms and markets such as the one in his old village. He can't imagine them fitting into his village; their clothes and hair and pink cheeks would make them too alien. He would advise them not to smile so much, or laugh or shout too loudly as they did when they ate their ice-creams and slid down the snowy slopes.

'Read, read,' his mother says so he makes some more words for her. *Look, it's raining, Jim,* and she says it back to him.

The boy looks at the dog, the cow, the chickens. Hears the sounds they make, though he doesn't make these sounds out loud. He would like to hear the dog bark. It would make a high sound because it is just a little dog. The chickens would make a deep clucking which would rise in pitch if they became agitated or afraid. In the past he has been guilty of chasing chickens, of enjoying the acceleration of their clucking as he ran after them. He has never chased a cow or any big animal. Not a donkey or a goat, though he has been tempted to do so. To run after any animal now seems improbable: not even Jim or Annie could do that in here.

When he reaches the end of the story the boy goes back to the start. It is easier to read it the second time around, to pronounce the words more confidently once he knows how the story ends. *It is Saturday and Jim and Annie are going to their uncle's farm.* What the boy would like to see in this story is a little furry rabbit. There has not been one in any story so far though Jim and Annie have seen tigers and elephants and horses and pigs. They have stretched their heads backwards to take in the height of a giraffe and laughed at the monkeys in their cages. Their uncle's farm would be the ideal place for a rabbit. There is plenty of grass under the apple trees. The rabbit might even eat one of the fallen apples, though the boy is not sure if this should be part of a rabbit's diet. He will have a rabbit one day, this is his dream, a white rabbit with long white ears through which you can see the pink flush of skin underneath. A nose as pink as Annie's and Jim's cheeks, and eyes as pink and glistening as the ice-cream they ate.

'Read,' his mother says and he pretends not to hear.

His rabbit will live in a neat box in which he will place clean straw each day. When the weather is good he will let his rabbit out to hop around on the grass. His fingers long for the touch of soft fur, thick and sweet-scented, the warm pulsing body of the animal underneath. In a market in his old country the market trader let him stroke a rabbit. He gazed into pink rabbit eyes fringed with long lashes and touched his own nose to the rabbit's twitching one. If he can afford it one day he will buy a boy and a girl rabbit and they will have many babies, and then, like Jim and Annie, they will have a farm.

Now his mother is making the sad sound she often makes, so low it is sometimes hard to hear it. He stares down at the book, at the primary brightness of it, not wanting to turn his head. It is the sound of a very low note from an ancient musical instrument or the deep growl of a wild dog. He has heard it so many times now he wonders if this is what links human beings to animals, some wild thing inside each person that attempts to escape through their mouths. In this place he has heard it rise from the throats of all the women but also from some of the men. They sit silently, sometimes they rock, and when they try to speak there comes instead this deep, terrible note, so low it could be the last breath of the dead. He waits until it has passed but then it comes again so he opens his book and reads more loudly.

What a lovely day to go to the farm, Annie. I hope the chickens have laid some eggs, Jim.

It has passed.

He hears the rustle of his mother rising. She touches her hand to his back, says, 'Come.' He puts the book neatly on the pile by his bed and follows her through the centre and outside into the sun. Some women are sitting under an awning and they call to his mother softly. 'Go,' she says, towards the swings that have been set up for the smallest children. 'Play.' He looks across at the children there, swinging slowly backwards and forwards in the heat. Can she not see he is too old for their games? The centre's children don't go high like Jim and Annie when they rode on the swings at the circus, their feet pointing upwards so you could see the soles of their shoes. He would rather go back inside and look at his books, but he wants to please his mother. He does not want her to growl again like an animal. When she is in the sun with the other women the sound, for the moment at least, goes away.

He walks instead to the centre's perimeter and looks towards the outer fence with the barbed wire on top. He says the name softly, 'Villawood'. There were woods here once, he decides, full of squirrels and foxes and rabbits and birds. Jim and Annie in their warm winter coats would have gathered chestnuts as they did in one of their books. From here he often listens to the sounds of passing cars and the voices of people queuing to come in to visit. There is nowhere secret here in which to hide a rabbit, even if he could ask a visitor to sneak one in for him. And there is so little grass there is nothing for a rabbit to eat.

He waits for his mother until the dinner bell. They eat then watch television. He reads his stories. They pray. Once he used to impress his teacher with each newly learned word and the way in which he understood Jim and Annie and the bright and free lives they led. Once he used to tell his teacher about the life he would lead when he was allowed to go with his mother to a new home, a farm, perhaps, with a cow and chickens and a dog and lots of rabbits, though the teacher told him that rabbits on farms are not popular in Australia. Or perhaps he and his mother could just live in a square house and a garden like those he saw from the bus when they brought them here. Villas, he decided, to go in the woods. But it has been so long he doesn't bother the teacher anymore with his dreams. Annie and Jim will remain the same age in the blue books with other children's messages scrawled across them but he is getting older and his dreams, like his memories of the village and its animals, the chickens and hardworking donkeys, the goats and rabbits, are beginning to fade. Jim and Annie will live their bright and simple lives, milking a cow, collecting the hens' eggs, stroking the pliant fur of a little dog who understands through the touch what a burden it is to be a human sometimes.

The lights are out and he calls goodnight to his mother. Her reply is soft. 'May God watch over you, my son.' He prays for her to sleep well too, free from nightmares, for what they have lost, for the dead, for the living. He prays for his longed-for rabbit.

Just as he is slipping towards sleep he hears again that low, desperate animal growl. Does it come from his mother? The whole building seems to sigh it. And then from his own throat he hears a more terrible sound. The cry of the rabbit as the market trader took it from its box for a customer and with one neat, sharp crack, broke its neck.

The Navigator

My generation navigated their way north as migrating birds are first pulled north, then south, all instinct tethered to season. After the constraints of high school, then university, we were drawn to places in which we would be different. We felt far too alike when we were at home. London was the most popular destination. Clive James, Germaine Greer, Robert Hughes: they'd led the dash a decade or two earlier, but in the early 1980s London still seemed a place in which an Australian could make a name for themselves. We went by ship in shared cabins on the lower decks, the more adventurous of us flying to Darwin then island-hopping to Indonesia and up to India. I travelled cautiously with a small canvas bag my mother had taken on her honeymoon. On her advice I packed it with easy-care clothes, things I could wash and hang out in my hotel bathroom on the elastic clothesline she put in the bag's inner pocket.

Now, of course, everyone comes to us – migrants, tourists, refugees in boats. They believe life will be better here, more fully lived and safer. It's a dice tossed towards shipwreck, towards haven, a terrible game played between people and the sea. When I was young I had the wanderlust of the traveller who has a safe home to return to. Australia seemed a sea-burdened place to me, so I was keen to visit a place that had no sea around it.

And so I left, my plane flying first over Botany Bay, retracing the voyages of the colony's first settlers two centuries earlier, before banking and heading across the continent's interior. There were times as I looked down on that dry red landscape, more sentimental than I should have been, maudlin after those glasses of departure wine, I suppose, that I thought the flat red country resembled a rolling inland sea. It stretched in waves, rose and dipped, the heat creating spume.

I travelled for two days through a landscape that could have been on the moon. I smiled at that comparison: the moon after all is also bedevilled by sea. Tranquillity, Crises, Serenity, Fecundity. The heat was a billowing curtain. Men and women were covered against sand. Dervishes swirled for the tourists as the sun went down, their white skirts making spinning tops of them. Swallows rose and dropped in the night air. A voice called the faithful to prayer. Fires grazed grilling meat. A hawker enticed, 'Mint tea, mint tea.' I walked slowly, my body finding a capacity for undulation I didn't know it had, a-sail amidst a long-gowned crowd who moved as though they had wheels instead of feet. I booked into a small but lovely place. Passed through a carved doorway, a tiled hall that opened into a little courtyard, tiled also, a fountain in its centre, and in each corner a potted date palm. A boy took my bag. The concierge beckoned me to a couch. Arabic coffee appeared, its scent of cardamom faint as the coffee was poured into tiny cups from a great height. I was impressed by the show. I laughed. The concierge was pleased. My passport was exchanged for a room key.

When I entered my room I saw my bag was already unpacked. I counted my clothes carefully in case of theft: three shirts, one pair of dressy trousers, a linen jacket. The red silk tie my mother had given me just before I left. I had a pair of espadrilles, a swimming costume, a sarong. These were arranged in neatly folded piles upon the bed. On my bedside table a jug of water wore a crochet hat. A saucer held two succulent dates. The window opened onto a balcony that looked into the buildings on the other side of the narrow street. Their shutters were closed against the heat and noise, but their louvres offered slits of light. I washed in a tiny bathroom tiled from floor to ceiling with small square turquoise tiles the colour of the country's missing sea. They could have been planed from a lump of lapis lazuli or turquoise; they caught the light, bounced, refracted, turning my mirror face blue. I cleaned my teeth and spat bottled water into a small brass basin resting on a cabinet inlaid with what might have been ivory, or plastic. The towels were soft and white. I spread out on a bed covered in white silk. My pillows were perfumed with sandalwood. I went out into the square at eleven, my ship body sailing from stall to stall. I passed men whose eyes narrowed as they sized me up. An adventurer. A spy. A tourist. I was all of these. My eyes stole secrets, my senses appropriated. My body was watchful, ready for adventure. The square knew it.

I had never been in a country so far inland. With no sea to navigate I needed a different compass. The land was all, the desert its only tide. It slouched, like Yeats's fabled lion towards Bethlehem. The hotel offered day trips and guides to show me the city's wonders – a fortress against the crusaders, a mosque of such exquisite shape and form; my body redefined itself, became more circular too, closer to some metaphysical state. I was offered a picnic with some Americans at an oasis. We went in four-wheel drives and rested under the date palms to eat from carefully packed picnic hampers. I was hounded by small children as I walked in the old town. In the daylight the square looked plain and unadorned as it awaited the night's transforming glow of firelight.

I woke and slept to the call to the faithful. Time ticked away to prayer. It was a full stop, a pause in my narrative. Each day a story, each night a slow promenade towards or away from adventure. I have heard it said that tourists are the most vulnerable people on earth. They want too much. They are too hungry for experience. They trust too easily. They let their guards down. I would add the caution that their senses are greedy. They grow fat and lazy and blowzy on too much experience. That's what it was like for me. I woke in silk, began each day with the cloying sweetness of dates and cardamom coffee, then set sail into a city that watched me as a lion watches its prey.

It is easy to exoticise the past, of course, now I'm back in Sydney. Outside are the red-tiled roofs of my neighbours' houses, their neat green gardens, their carports. It's quiet here during the day and quiet at night. I catch a train into the city to a concert or a film. My train clatters across the Harbour Bridge, the water glimpsed below us. I meet friends in bars that overlook the harbour. I walk through the eloquence of a crushed cellophane twilight. The city's high-rise buildings cling to the water's edge, so does the Opera House but it is all rather dull in comparison with the mess and swirl of a youth spent looking for something.

On my third night in the hotel – by then the staff were a family of sorts – I saw that the shutters across the way were open and that a young man was standing there looking towards where I was lying on my bed. He watched for a moment before going inside. The shutters closed behind him. A few nights later I saw him on the square, some beads in his hand, flicked backwards and forwards impatiently like the tail of a cow pestered by flies. His eyes met mine in recognition, then he turned to his friends and said something. They looked towards me too, four impossibly handsome youths in casual white shirts. I browsed a stall of tooled leather bags, examined a footstool bearing the shape of a camel. In the mirror of a portable barber shop, men sitting before it on upturned fruit crates, I saw he was following me.

Time seemed to pass differently after that. I was on a stage and he was my audience. 'Monsieur,' a hawker called, mistaking me for French.

I waved a dismissive hand. 'No thanks.'

'Sir,' he called now. 'Sir. Very nice.' He pointed towards some red-and-black woven shawls. 'For your mother, sir, or your wife.'

I walked towards the square's darker corners, each time turning back towards the light. The young man followed, light to dark, then back to light, as I stood before a brazier on which a goat was roasting. At one point the man was so close I could smell his cologne above the rich scent of roasting meat. I felt his breath on the back of my neck, warm and soft as one expects of languid night. A trio of musicians struck up, a flat, oddly rhythmic piece to which men began to clap. Some little boys, pretend dervishes, began to swirl about. Their fathers called them to be still. Laughter. The square was a world of men immersed in the night. This is the life, I thought. I am really alive here.

I did not see the young man again for almost a week. I booked another fortnight at the hotel. It wasn't expensive and I wasn't bound by any schedules. I spent time exploring the old city, avoiding the children with outstretched hands, stopping in doorways to look up at the impossible height of the mud-brick buildings, some still bearing a defaced crusaders' cross.

One night I came home late and, switching on my light, saw that the shutters opposite were open and the room lit up. I immediately turned my light off, heard some laughter percolating up from the street below. He must have seen me, because he came to the window and looked towards where I stood in the dark. He turned away and I thought, he'll close the shutters now, but he didn't. He stood in the centre of his room and I slid through the dark of mine towards my balcony. I opened the doors and stepped out.

I waited, the air hot and dry and full with the desert, so close the sand sometimes hissed along the street. I heard it if I was awake in the night, sliding, hissing its viper path through the town. He saw me. He turned and slowly he took off his clothes. I won't describe the shock of it. His beauty, what he did after that as I continued to watch. He lay down on his bed and turned off his light and I lay down on mine. That is how we spent our first night together and the following five nights.

My doctor says, 'You are elderly, you mustn't expect too much of your body now.'

'Misspent youth?' I laugh.

'You are lucky that you visited places that are wartorn while they were peaceful and you had the chance. You are also lucky to live in a place like this.'

Like this? I look again at the hot red roofs, the big back-yards with their jacarandas and Hills hoists and barbeques. Royal North Hospital is visible on the ridge of the Pacific Highway and beyond it the harbour ebbs and flows.

I didn't see the young man on his balcony or in the square for a while, though I passed his friends often enough. One night one of them called to me. 'Sir.' I nodded, not knowing what else I could do. My young man wasn't with them and I was not brave enough to ask where he was. I thought I might leave on the weekend. The city and the desert had shown off all their charms. I was surprisingly tired though I was sleeping well.

Then one night his light was on again and I went out onto my balcony and stood and waited. He didn't do what he usually did. Instead he came onto his balcony, so close in the narrow street. He made a sound, a kiss, a whistle, a hiss like the invading sand. He raised his hand and moved it to mimic opening a door. He pointed to the door of my room, made the movement again and then beckoned. He was asking me to throw him my key. 'No.' I shook my head. He pleaded with his hands, an amusing play I'd seen stall vendors use as they bargained. 'Please, sir, please.' And so we played – please, no, please, no. I wanted him. Something reckless in me gnawed through my self-restraint. I threw the key and waited.

It seemed an eternity before he arrived, and I found out much later it was because the concierge had detained him in the courtyard, at the couch where on my first night I'd tasted the coffee. He'd sweet-talked the concierge, though, and here he was, his thick dark curls more shiny than I'd been able to see from a distance. He seemed shy now, not like the young man I'd watched display himself. I took his hand and drew him into the room. We didn't talk. The bed awaited us and its cool, white silk sheets. He looked around. Smiled when he saw how much I saw of his room.

Before he left early the next morning he told me his name was Hassan. Later I saw him dressing in his room across the way, preparing his morning coffee. He made a lewd gesture with his hips and I made the same one back. I felt the pleasure again of our night. No rest. No restrictions. I wondered how his lips might taste now he had drunk some coffee. The hotel boy arrived with my breakfast and as he placed the tray on the chest at the end of my bed, he looked towards the room opposite, then he closed the shutters and said, 'It is very windy today. Sir, please, no sand in your room.'

I stayed in the city with no sea for three months, slowly depleting my travel money. I had planned a lot – a long trip through the Middle East, through Turkey and Eastern Europe, arriving in London as the warmer weather came, the only way to endure London, my Australian friends had said. Hassan and I spent nights in my room, the concierge watchful but the room-service boy no less friendly. Sometimes a beautiful new servant would arrive at my door for no reason other than to dust away invisible sand or check whether I needed fresh towels.

No. I wanted nothing. I had all that I needed.

I knew I was in love by the fifth week. My knees trembled whenever I saw Hassan. My heart raced. He took me to new places in the old town, to abandoned buildings on the edge of the desert, their rough mudbricks pressing patterns into my bare skin when we made love. I bought him new clothes, a second-hand motor scooter. His mother needed some cash and I was happy to help. His brother wanted to go to Ankara to school. I helped with his school fees. Then one day Hassan was gone. I searched the square for him. Trawled the narrow streets of the old town. I spent more and more time in my room, my eyes fixed on his closed shutters.

A letter was delivered to the hotel. It was from his brother. 'Please to contact me urgently.' I tried the number. I must have misread the writing because the phone always rang out. I showed it to the concierge. He gave me a look that resided somewhere between humour and pity. He took the letter from me and said he'd try to call. I didn't see the letter again and when I asked for it he explained that he'd called and that my friend had gone to Jordan.

'To Jordan?'

'Yes. He has gone to Jordan on family business.'

The doctor asks how my sex life is going. 'Comfortable,' I say. 'A bit dull. You know what it's like when you've been with someone as long as Martin and I have been together.'

He smiles. Writes something in my file.

'I'm just pleased Martin is prepared to put up with me.'

That smile again. He says, 'All relationships are based on compromise.' Ah, yes, I think, but there's compromise and being compromised.

I didn't hear from Hassan again and there was nothing to keep me in the city now all its joys were over. Inexplicably, I found myself longing for water, for the sea, for wide and turbulent oceans. I wanted to stand before a roaring surf and feel its salt pelt my skin. I wanted to stand up to my neck in it, to be buffeted and tossed. I was offered a lift with some young German tourists who were heading north in a beat-up kombi. I went with them and arrived in Munich a few weeks later.

'Please give my friend this address in Sydney if he comes to ask,' I said to the hotel manager before I left.

'Of course,' he said and I had no reason not to believe him.

After a year with a law firm in London, I was surprised by the siren call of Sydney. London was dull, still too closely bound to the past. It seemed a pop-up picture book place of changing guards and palaces and beefeaters and camera-tethered tourists. I was sick of England's obsession with class, the way a patronising tone crept into a client's voice when they heard my Australian accent. 'Antipodean' was a word I didn't react to well. I wanted some sunshine, and the easy informality of Australia.

I arrived home on a hot March day – not quite summer, not quite autumn. This time the plane flew from the west, tracking over the Blue Mountains, circling north towards Berowra before following the bays and inlets of the northern side of the harbour. It passed over my mother's house and the school I'd attended, North Sydney, the grinning, lunatic face of Luna Park's gate just visible before we banked again and slid down to the airport.

A pile of letters was waiting at my mother's, all of them postmarked with the name of the city in which I'd discovered Hassan and a part of myself I hadn't before understood. That place was as much about sand and sea as it was about love, I'd decided, as I'd worked through London's long and gloomy winter. It was about the way water shapes one self and sand shapes another. They come together. They are worlds apart. 'I am Hassan's brother,' the first letter read. 'He is dying of AIDS and you must help him.'

AIDS, I thought. I don't have AIDS. I tore open the other eight letters and read them all quickly. 'He is dying, Michael. You must help him.' And then in the last letter, dated some six months after the first. 'He has died, sir. Please help us.'

The doctor says it's all a nonsense. I have become paranoid about something impossible. I never had AIDS. I would never get it. I am too careful, too committed to safe sex. 'Are you sure it isn't a scam?' he continues to ask. 'How much money have you sent these people now? What is it? Twenty years?'

'More like thirty.'

He sighs. He has heard the story before. Martin has told him too, about the letters from a bombed place, the pleading to let them send their grandchildren to us, for safety.

I have tried to explain it to Hassan's people, have paid translators to make my meaning very clear. I can't explain how it works to Martin or the doctor either. Since the late 1980s I have sent thousands of dollars, first to his mother and brother, then to his nieces and nephews, now to some 'grand-children'. I have changed my will so that one day the family may have enough to free themselves, to travel to a place where there are no bombs or rifles or raids. Given the current state of the region, I have no idea where that might be. I have told them there is no hope of migration to Australia.

Martin is bemused rather than condemning. He knows that life is full of these sad tricks.

Hassan wanted to know where I lived and what I did. He believed one day he might be free to migrate. 'You are a lawyer? So your family is rich?'

'No,' I said.

'But richer than people here?'

We looked around the square at the polyglot crowd, the laughter and music. 'It depends on how you define *rich*,' I said foolishly.

I explained that migration wasn't as simple as he thought. There were rules and expectations, regulations and economic imperatives. Countries like Australia were looking for qualified migrants like engineers and doctors and teachers. He was none of those things.

The doctor is finished. He closes my file, gives me a gentle pat on the knee. 'You're as fit as a fiddle for a man of your age. Keep it up.'

I stand. 'I'll tell Martin. He likes to keep me on a regime.'

I walk outside onto Military Road, clogged at this time of the afternoon with buses and cars. I turn towards our street, our house with its tropical garden and snatches of turquoise harbour. Tonight Martin and I will dine at a new restaurant on the water. I'll slip, as I always do, into a sea reverie. Hassan always floats through it, his face as bright and young as it was all those years ago.

My country. His country. Our bodies somewhere in between. I realised back then that I knew the sea too well and Hassan knew it too little. He may well still be alive. If he is I hope he remembers me fondly. I hope he understands what happens when you leave something behind and navigate towards something else. There comes a time when the navigation is all; it really doesn't matter if you never find what you are seeking.

Hell Comes, Hell Goes

It's hell. Weirdo hell. The cops look at you, people walk away. You got to live it. You know what I mean? Last time I was in Muswellbrook. Ever been there? Don't bother. It's a shithole. I was on the railway station and this guy comes up to me and says, 'Why don't you get a job?'

I'd just worked my arse off for two weeks fixing roads for the council. Couldn't stop for a sec without some bastard ringing the council and saying, 'You know those blokes up on the Singleton Road? Well, they're *not working*.' The foreman would come out to check we weren't slacking. 'I'll lay you off if you slack.' What did he think we were, a bloody chain gang or something? I got a room at the pub. I paid in advance. I was at the depot on time every day. Then some old woman would see you having a smoke. One old bird even came to her gate and watched us work. I'd like to have flattened her with the shovel. That would have taught her a lesson. So after two weeks the foreman says, 'That's it, boys, job's done.' I was going to go down and see my sister at Beeni but I'd been there a few months before. She's a bit weird too, man. Should see the poetry she writes. It runs in the family. Being weird, I mean – not poetry. So I worked my arse off for two weeks, paid the hotel. Bought stuff in town and some old cunt says, 'You should get a job.' Old people piss me off. Always down on younger people. It's because they don't have enough to do. They get up. They fiddle around. They watch TV. They go to bed. Then they die.

Anyway. I said to this bloke on the station, 'You speak to me like that again and you'll regret it.' He didn't even have the good sense to walk away. He just stood in front of me with his hands on his hips. If I'd had the shovel I tell you he'd have been dead meat. I lowered my voice till it was real menacing, then I said, 'Piss off, you stupid old fool.' He moved off then. I thought he'd gone to get the cops or someone who works on the station but they don't have people working on country stations anymore. The train came and he got in the front carriage and I got in the last one. He got off at Broadmeadow. He gave me a dirty look as he went past where I was sitting.

So when we got to Gosford I thought, will I or won't I? Lizzie doesn't like surprises so I stayed on the train. She's always fussing. 'You taking your meds? You eating enough? What happened to your tooth? When did you last have a bath? Why do you talk like that? We went to good schools. Why do you talk like a…?' She couldn't find the right word so I helped her out. Fuckwit? Dickhead? Nut case? Sisters, man. I just said, 'Yeah, yeah, all's good.' What should I have said? 'I can talk as posh as you, mate. It's just when the voices take over that I…blah blah…' Yeah, sure.

Lizzie is like a mother. She feeds me. She's a great cook. Better than any shearers' cook and they're pretty good. But after a while being on an island really freaks you out. Fuck, man. It's like hell with nowhere to run. 'Why are you going? Stay here, Danny.'

'No,' I said last time I was there. 'I got work up in New England.' She was pleased with that. She reckons work is all I need to keep my mind off things. I've tried to explain. It's not like that. Madness travels with you. Wouldn't matter what you were doing or where.

That's why I stayed on the train this time and went down to Central and I rang a bloke I know in the Riverina and he said, 'Come down and do some picking because we can't get workers other than wogs and refos.' He talks like that but he doesn't mean it. He's not racist or anything. So I go down to Leeton and he picks me up and some other blokes from the train and drives us here. End of story. There was one bloke. Black. 'What's your name?' I said. 'Where did you come from?'

'Axmed,' he said. 'My name means most praised. I have come here from Somalia. Do you know where that is?'

He said it just like that, man. Real serious, straight-faced.

'Yeah, sort of. It's in Africa, right?'

And he says, 'Africa is a very big place. Somalia is at the end of the Red Sea, at the top. It is NORTH Africa.'

I wanted to laugh. I said, 'You ever pick fruit before?'

'No. Not in my country. Not in any other place. I was a teacher.'

So I told him. I said, 'Well, there's a first time for every-thing, isn't there?'

Like voices, right? Shit, man, the first time I heard voices I thought I'd gone to hell and back. Cops picked me up and put me in a cell. I thought they were fucking aliens with antennas growing out of their heads. Then they took me to an admission centre. I didn't have any ID but they scheduled me anyway. Some bird came and checked me out and said, go ahead, and next thing I knew I was in the loony bin and they were giving me drugs and stuff. I was seeing other things by then, this creepy bloke with a big black mask. He kept calling me to him and I knew if I went I'd be dead as a dodo so I ran and hid but I could hear him calling. *Danny. Danny. I'll find you.* Man, that was weird.

This place isn't bad. Tucker's good. The sheds are okay. Mattresses are clean. No fleas or bed bugs. Beats working for a council, I tell you. You get to eat a lot of fruit. I picked double my quota of fruit today. How about you? This Axmed, he's been struggling. 'How you going, Ax? How's the picking?'

You know what he said? 'I am slow at picking, Daniel. I am not good at it.'

I had to laugh. No one much's called me Daniel since I was a nipper. Well, doctors have but that doesn't count. 'Cheer up, Ax. You'll get the hang of it soon enough. You get a kind of rhythm going, know what I mean?'

Today I was stung by a wasp. Know what that's like? It hurt like hell. I managed to kill it, though. Served the fucker right. You go for me and you're gone. I once saw giant wasps too. Not sure what was worse, the bloke in the black mask or giant wasps coming after me. Noise like a bloody jet engine. Stinger like a lance, if they got you they'd run you through. I told Axmed about it at lunch – salad sandwiches today. Apple juice. More fruit than you want. You know what Axmed said? 'There were men in my country with machetes who chopped people apart. It was like animals in an abattoir. Terrible. Women and babies too.' Whoa. That a hallucination, mate, or are you talking for real? Cause if it's real I reckon at least you can run away from them, right? You made it here, which has got to be good, hasn't it? Better than getting chopped apart by a wild pack of men. But me, mate? Hallucinations travel with you. There's no escaping them.

This morning I saw Axmed up a ladder. I could hardly make him out in all the green leaves. The sky above him was really blue. Blue skies used to scare me once, the earth spinning too. If you think too much about it, you get dizzy. It's true! The heat was shit by nine. I was sweating like the proverbial. I felt weird every time I climbed the ladder. I could see Axmed down the row working on his trees. We were picking peaches today and the air smelled of ripening fruit. Axmed looked odd, wavy like a heatwave. His skin was turning blue. He climbed his ladder, balancing carefully against the branches. Furry to the touch, white peaches. See? My uncle made some pots that colour once. Soft pink, like skin. Lizzie's still got them. Anyway, Axmed picked up his full bag and took his fruit to the crate. I shouted, 'Watch they don't cheat you, Ax!'

'Shut up, ya dickhead.' That was the boss. He's always calling me a dickhead. No-hoper. Fuckwit. If I owned an orchard I'd give the fruit a bit longer, I told him. The peaches are too hard. Fruit has to travel but it doesn't taste as good when it's rock hard. Still, us pickers can eat the overripe stuff, ripe fruit fresh from the tree. Supermarkets don't know what they're missing.

Lunch was served under the trees. Some of the blokes went off to pray first. You see them all hours with their arses in the air. I sat down and waited for the food. It's always good. They serve water and juice. Most of the blokes don't drink alcohol anyway and I'm not allowed to drink it with my meds. You could fall out of a bloody tree if you weren't careful, it's dangerous, fruit picking. You sometimes forget you're on a ladder and step off and, wham, broken leg or arm before you know it. I've seen it happen but it's never happened to me.

Axmed was at the other end of the table. I waved and he nodded with that slow downward movement of his head. It's both dignified and irritating at the same time, if you get my drift. If I ever get into a state again I'll want to deck him, that's for sure. There's just something too neat about him. His clothes, his hair, that black skin stretched tight over his facial bones. He's a bit evil, turning blue like he is. He's going a funny colour like the man in the mask. His voice sounds like it's coming from a long way away, then it gets really loud. Shit, I dread that man in the dream. He's really creepy. The doctor at the hospital said I backed into a corner and put my hands over my head when I saw him. Too right I did, I said. That black fucker was going to kill me. Under his mask he's a heaving mass of something evil, worms or wasps or pus. Maybe he's something even more terrifying, something inside all of us waiting to get out and hack up the whole world with a machete. The doctor just patted me on the back. 'There's no one with machetes here, Daniel. We live in one of the safest places on this earth. Stay on your meds, okay? Eat well. Exercise. But above all look after yourself and make sure your prescription is filled.'

I looked that doctor straight in the eye. 'Sure, mate,' I said. 'I always do.' He laughed. Sceptical. They all are.

I wanted to grab him by the neck of his shirt. I wanted to say, I was a kid once. I was a little boy. I was normal then. My dad and my mum, Lizzie and me, we were always going to beaches. Shit, we loved the sea. You can forget anything at a beach. Water swallows you. It washes away all your sins. It washes away bad dreams. We used to make things out of sand – castles, cars. Lizzie and me made a mermaid once. We were bloody good. If they'd had sandcastle competitions we'd have won them, that's for sure. We used to be happy, if you know what I mean. Real happiness. Not that crap they tell you about on TV. Not on-meds happiness. Fuck that. That's not happy. That's a pretend way to be. You're plastic. You're cellophane. You're Glad Wrap. You're looking at the world from behind a big glass wall. Lizzie's got the right idea. Write stuff. Write nice words that rhyme and look like something on a page. Not black masks or wasps. Words that could be the sea or an apple tree in blossom or the soft velvety skin of a peach.

See. I can be just as poetic as my sister. Hey, Abdul. Imran. Get on with it. Prayer time's over, mate, we're hungry. You must have sucked up to him in the sky long enough by now. Come on, you lazy arseholes, we've got to eat before we start picking again.

'Shut it, Danny, or you're out of here.'

'Yeah. Yeah, boss. Keep your daks on. I'm only mucking around. They know it's a joke, don't you? Yeah, see.'

Back to picking at one. It's the wrong time of day for it. The afternoon heat is heavy, my stomach's too full. I'm as furry as one of the peaches. I'm thirsty and want a swim. That'll teach me to think about the beach. I didn't take my meds last night. They make me too dizzy on the ladder.

The world gets wavy without them. But things taste better. These peaches are so sweet. If I eat any more I'll get the runs.

Hey, Axmed, look at this. Come on, take a gander. I can balance a peach on the end of my nose, like a seal. Not funny? What are you staring at? Hey, Ax. Axie. Where you going? Going to get a machete, mate, axe, machete, get it? Hey, saw. Hey, hammer. Where you going? Hey, hey. Don't give me that dirty look. I don't like that black mask. You're turning blue. Axmed. Axxxxxy. You heard me. Come here, no, come on. Come here, mate.

Love

His best friend, Amy, told him he represented her mother. He said, 'But I'm a man.'

Amy replied, 'It doesn't matter, Dave. It's symbolic.' She paused to look at some handbags in the window of Scally and Trombone. 'A mother can be any gender.'

They went into the new cafe on the corner of Johnston and Brunswick streets and sat by the window. A waiter came over. Cute. He had a nice tight little arse. Normally Dave would have said something about him to Amy but after the mother stuff he thought, fuck you, I'm keeping my erotic fantasies to myself.

Amy stirred her coffee and raised it to her mouth. She sighed and said, 'I'm sorry, Dave, I can't be friends with you anymore. I have to break free from all the mother figures in my life.'

Outside, a tram clattered along Brunswick Street. The shock of Amy's announcement had caused Dave's mouth to open. I must look like a goldfish, he thought, my mouth a perfect O. Then he decided she had to be joking. That was it, she was mucking around.

'Okay,' he said. 'As long as I'm a glamorous *Mommie Dearest* like Joan Collins – or was it Joan Crawford?'

Amy's face was stern as she put her coffee down. 'I'm not joking, Dave. I have to get away from friends who represent the negative aspects of my life, namely my mother.'

'What's that supposed to mean?'

Amy answered slowly, enunciating each word as though he was some low-intelligence kid. 'My psychiatrist...says...I have...to reject...those people in my life...who represent... my mother. I'm sorry, Dave, but she says you're one of them.'

'How does she know? She's never met me.'

Amy had the grace to look guilty. 'I tell her about you.'

'Why?'

'I talk about everyone.'

'Your real mother?'

'Of course.'

'But what have you said to the doctor about me? How can she know what I'm like if she's never met me?'

Amy shrugged and signalled to the waiter to bring over two more coffees. 'I tell her about all my friends.' She spread her arms wide to take in their table, the cafe, Fitzroy, the Saturday crowds of shoppers outside. 'About all this.'

'Your sex life?'

'Yes. And yours.' She gave one of her grim little smiles.

Dave sighed. Amy's sex life was hell. It always had been, but his – well, his was pretty good. Only last week he'd finally summoned the courage to go out into the alley with Jake, a man he always danced with at the club. They'd gone to the wall where the Banksy was supposed to have been painted – a mouse running up a drainpipe. Not that he and Jake were thinking about that at the time. Jake had long eyelashes and a mouth that tasted of wine, and a hard, flat six-pack stomach, and a cock just as hard. The remembered pleasure flowed down Dave's spine like something molten.

Amy was looking around the cafe as though she was hoping to pick up someone too. She'd been online dating for the past few years. She got upset when the dates never went past the first night. Dave had given her his views on that. It was a mistake to always sleep with the guy on the first night. He said, 'There's no seduction in that, no tease. String them along a bit. Do the romantic thing with dinners and flowers and getting to know all about them before you fuck them.'

Amy was not convinced. 'I thought gay men were supposed to just jump into bed with anyone. I thought you liked to just go for it.'

Go for it? he'd thought at the time. If only you knew.

As the coffee machine huffed and puffed he again remembered the alley. His spine tingled. He was getting hard. He and Jake had sashayed around one another at the bar for weeks before getting hot on the dance floor, weaving and flirting and brushing their bodies against one another. They were like a matador and a bull, fencers keen on penetration, steeplejacks climbing a bloody tall steeple. Metaphors failed him. Jake liked dry white wine. He sometimes ate the complimentary peanuts as he waited at the bar. He smelled of aftershave – Dave had never been able to work out which one – a musky smell, pampered and confident. Then came the more intimate touching, the words of seduction shouted over the music, the drinks taken back to the club's leather armchairs, the alley outside and Jake's urgent kisses.

Dave looked around the cafe. He knew most of the people. Heidi from the bookshop had popped in for a takeaway coffee. A young couple he recognised from his block of flats were ordering babycinos for their kids. The two gay men from the homewares shop were over by the door. He'd been clocking their relationship for the past six weeks. How long had they been a couple? He'd fancied the muscular one since he'd first seen him dressing the shop window.

Amy made a funny little noise in her throat. She might have been choking, or perhaps he just wished she were. 'Dave, I don't mean to be cruel. I just can't see you anymore.'

He heard the panic in his voice as he spoke. 'But we've been friends since I arrived in Melbourne.'

She was already rifling around her bag for her purse. 'I'll pay for these.'

So determined was her tone he let her be. He let her pull her coat off the back of her chair without helping her put it on. Let her walk out the door and turn towards Collingwood. What else can you do when someone says you represent their mother? He stared into the cafe's mirrored wall, deep into his own eyes. No mother looked back, though he could see the family resemblance, his mother's dark hair, her olive skin, her propensity for laughter lines around her eyes. He thought about all the vile mothers he could muster. Joan Crawford, certainly. She at least had glamour. Judy Garland. Too tragic. Margaret Thatcher? Her nasty politics seemed to desex her; he certainly couldn't imagine her enjoying moments of maternal tenderness. The mother in *Psycho*? He shivered. If he rang Amy later would she tell him when this metamorphosis had happened? Was it after they went up to Sydney for Mardi Gras and he put on red lipstick and a red wig? She'd told him her mother was a redhead when she was young. Was it when they were on South Melbourne beach and he'd lectured her about freckles and the dangers of melanoma? Drinking cocktails together at Double Happiness in Chinatown? Was it when he confessed he was falling in love with Jake? He'd told her everything about his sex life until then. The long, slow penetrating sex with a former boyfriend, Steve; the soapy showers afterwards, one when Steve pushed him against the tiles and knelt down in front of him and let his lips graze Dave's inner thighs as the water played gently on them and Steve worked his way slowly, determinedly, up and up. He hadn't told her about Jake, though. Their love was different. There was something fragile and melting in it. The wrong move and it might all disappear.

Dave pulled himself back into the cafe. He and Amy had always done the fun things together that a nice mother might do with her daughter, or his kind of mother with her kind of son. He ordered another coffee and sat for a while, stirring it slowly. Amy had always had a difficult relationship with her mother but he'd liked Mrs Griffiths from the very first time he'd met her. He could never say that to Amy, of course. Mothers were to be experienced in certain and specific ways by their children. Friends generally saw only the best of them and that didn't quite count. He'd been over to the Griffiths' house in Kew lots of times, mostly when Amy needed to pick up something she'd left with her parents – a pot plant that needed to be watered when she was on holidays, a hem that needed taking up on a new dress – Mrs Griffiths was very good at sewing and mending.

Another time he'd gone with Amy to a Sunday lunch, a birthday celebration that Amy attended as a duty, the real one with friends a few days later. Her mother's gift had been a hand-knitted sweater that he'd liked a lot and said so. Mrs Griffiths surprised him a few weeks later with an express post parcel containing a scarf for him in the same wool, dark and soft and red. He wore it to the bar that night and Jake ran his hands along it, hooking it around his fingers and pulling Dave towards him for a kiss. 'Is this *pure* wool?' Jake asked, his emphasis on pure, and Dave felt his cock harden very impurely, his face flush as red as the scarf. 'I think so,' he whispered, his face close to Jake's ear.

Amy was less impressed with the gift. 'Emotional blackmail,' she called it. 'Colonising my friends.' Dave sent Mrs Griffiths a thank-you note anyway and wore the scarf all winter. Then one Sunday evening as he and Amy were crossing Princes Bridge after a concert at Southbank, Amy pulled the scarf from his neck and tossed it into the Yarra. They'd watched it fall in a long, curious line like a question mark, like it was asking him why it had been discarded.

'I've been dying to do that ever since my mother gave it to you,' she said.

Dave was so shocked he was unable to answer. He just watched the scarf float towards Williamstown, a soggy, dark red streak.

Dave paid the waiter and left, smiling a greeting to the homewares men as he passed them. He'd go to a movie at the Kino or the Nova, though he hadn't checked the programs so he didn't know what was on. Carlton, he decided. It was an easy walk and if none of the movies appealed he'd wander the clothes shops. He hadn't intended spending a Saturday alone but he didn't feel like calling anyone about their Saturday night plans. He might call Jake, and then again he mightn't. He'd been going to poke around the furniture shops of Johnston Street with Amy, walk up to Northcote afterwards, to an early dinner at their favourite Turkish restaurant. Jake. Not Jake. No, he'd better not call him. Sex. Love. Surely Jake wanted both? Oh well, he thought, shrugging at his reflection in a shop window. Amy's words hit him again. *You represent my mother.* He straightened his shoulders.

As he walked he thought about their friendship. He'd known Amy for six years. They'd been introduced just after he arrived from Sydney. She'd flirted with him at first, doing that thing he'd seen her do with other available men. She smiled a lot, her conversation sometimes veering towards the nasty. She said it turned men on if women were provocative with them. One day, when she'd asked him home to a special dinner he'd said gently, 'I can't that night, I have a date with a man from work,' and the light bulb went on in her eyes. She was okay after that. 'My sexless friend,' she called him. 'My gay friend, Dave.' Had she told her mother? He'd often wondered.

He and Amy had done the walk to Carlton numerous times over the years, on their way to films or dinners with friends, arguing, sharing secrets, his early homesickness assuaged by entrée to Amy's life, and to outings uniquely Melbourne. Australian Rules, Sunday lunches in St Kilda, shopping-trolley promenades through Victoria Market, eating brunch at a sausage stall – Weisswurst, onions on a doughy white bun – while being serenaded by a busker. There was nothing like it in Sydney, he'd told her, and Amy laughed and said no, there was nowhere in Sydney like Vic Market.

In Rathdowne Street he stopped outside a second-hand shop, attracted by a tweed jacket which carried a history of wealth in its tailoring. Beside it an old television was showing some news, boats of refugees drowning. He rarely watched TV these days. It was too depressing. There were too many bad news stories about murders and robberies and refugee boats in which whole families died. As he watched this latest group he thought about Sydney Harbour and its yellow-and-green ferries, the harbour water silky as it brushed against the steps by the Opera House. It wasn't homesickness, exactly, it was more tactile than that. He wanted to take Jake to Sydney so they could experience it together, its water and sandstone buildings and frangipani trees and double-decker trains, and for the first time in ages he really missed his mother.

When he arrived at the Nova he scanned the program and decided on the latest Clint Eastwood film, *Gran Torino*. He queued with middle-aged, middle-class women who reminded him of his mother, girlfriends doing what girlfriends do on a Saturday afternoon. He followed them upstairs to wait for the theatre to open and eavesdropped on their conversations. They all seemed to be talking about their kids.

He found it difficult to concentrate on the film: it was too pat, too neat a fairytale about redemption. He glanced around the dark cinema at the rapt faces, the air scented with popcorn. The last time he was up in Sydney his mother had offered her own version of a fairytale. He'd gone over to her flat, the harbour dancing distantly outside her windows, sequinned by the sun. 'I have something to tell you,' he said.

She was making coffee and warming the croissants he'd picked up at the French bakery in Darlinghurst Road. She smiled and said, 'I think I know what it is.'

He'd been silenced by that for a moment but went on nervously. 'I'm gay.'

And his mother said, 'Oh, sweetheart, I've known that since you were fourteen.'

'You have?'

She nodded. 'Mothers do know these things.'

'But you didn't say anything.'

'Why would I? It was up to you to tell me.'

He could hear the accusation in his voice as he said, 'If you'd let me know earlier I'd have felt easier with it.'

'Would you, sweetie?'

'Yes, I think so.'

'Oh well, we've both reached the same place now. Jam and butter or just plain?'

'Jam.'

'Raspberry or strawberry?'

'Raspberry.'

They'd sat in the sunshine and watched the shadows move across the blocks of flats between them and the harbour, like soldiers resolutely marching. She'd touched his shoulder as she got up to take his cup. 'And is there anyone special?'

'No,' he fibbed, hoping she wasn't going to give him a lecture about safe sex.

'What about you, Mum? Have you met anyone nice?'

'No, but I had a party here last week.'

'And?'

'It was lovely. We all drank too much, of course.'

He feigned shock.

'I'm pleased for you,' she said again. 'I hope you meet someone you can have a good relationship with.'

What would he tell his mother about Amy? His mum was just as likely to tell him she'd never liked her. She'd never have told him that to his face, though, because people must be free to be friends with whomever they choose. What would she think of Jake?

The women were standing in small groups debating the film, deciding where to go for dinner. He would have liked to discuss *Gran Torino* with Amy right now. She was so good at deconstructing film narratives and she was up on the latest reviews. She always had an opinion about actors, and talked about them as if they were her best friends. It was disconcerting when she talked about Clint Eastwood like that, or Brad Pitt or George Clooney. He walked out into the late afternoon. The sun had gilded the plane trees on Lygon Street and the people sitting at the outdoor tables wore halos of golden light. He stood for a moment debating whether to walk into the city or back to Northcote. Should he ring Jake? Should he play it cool? He mustn't be too earnest, too determined, too much in love.

'Dave!'

Some men sat at one of the tables outside Tiamo, and one of them was Jake. Dave walked over slowly, looking carefully at the group. 'Jake. What a coincidence.'

'Isn't it. Sit down,' Jake said, giving him a hug. 'Have a drink with us.'

All around him the chatter of people, the loud boom-beat from the passing cars, Italian youths claiming their street, kids and old people, crows plane-tree hopping. Dave took a long swig of beer and let Jake introduce him to his friends, thinking how handsome Jake looked in his crisp blue shirt, his smile so welcoming, hands that would later trace the outline of his thighs, their mouths lip to lip. He was anticipating a good night after all, and something to announce to his mother when he called her the next day.

Love: there, he had called it at last. He would tell her he was in *love*.

The Rat Inside

Debra Murdoch loves going to the shopping mall on pension day. So many people shopping. She smiles at her reflection in a shop window. Hair neat. Nice new tartan skirt. Her arthritic toes mean she has to wear sensible lace-up shoes but that doesn't matter because most of the other old women are wearing them too. The mall is so vast she could spend a whole day just moving from floor to floor, stopping to look at the teardrop fountain, the junctions of the aisles where benches have been placed in case you get tired. There are signs too – *Toilets, Car Park A, Car Park B, Myer, David Jones, the International Food Court*. She pauses under a large potted palm and looks at a new sign. *Get Hai on Bali this week. Try our Indonesian specials in the food court. Look for the palm tree emblem for big discounts.* The mall's piped music sounds Asian too. She's never been to Bali, though she knows lots of people who have.

Debra, Debbie, Deb, she chides herself. Stop preening in the shop windows. Stop reassuring yourself. Despite what old women think, we don't *really* become invisible. We're still flesh and blood in sensible shoes, sensible haircuts and clothes. Move to the bookshop now, that's the girl. Lovely books, lovely covers, the blurbs on the back quite tantalising, especially the crime ones. Do people really get murdered like that? Do the police *really* treat one another as nastily as they do on TV? Goodness me, I hope not. Into the chemist for a free squirt of perfume, *Chanel No. 5. L'Air du Temps*. Girlhood perfume all over again. A favourite back in adolescence: *Je Reviens*. I will return. Such a pretty name.

She calls, 'Hello, Norma. Lovely day for shopping. Kids gone back to Melbourne? Nice to see them, isn't it, but nice when they go. Love to your Ernie. Bye bye.'

Time for a coffee? Michel's for a tarte au citron? A Paris-Brest. Didn't the boys at school laugh at *that*. The odious Kevin Richardson. The disgusting Paul Sedwick. They're probably grandfathers by now.

'Hello, Bert. I haven't seen you for a while.'

She straightens her skirt in the window of a shop that sells candles and scented oils and soaps so strongly perfumed they mark this corner of the mall with a very peculiar odour. She always knows when she's near the shop, that's for certain. It's a scent of old-fashioned lollies like sugar bananas and flying saucers and jelly babies. Of lavender and lemons. Reflected in the shop window her tartan skirt looks jaunty. Black Watch tartan, no less, with a big silver kilt pin. She had one just like it when she was five or six. A matching beret too. Children then were meant to be seen but not heard. Funny, these days, that old women are meant to be the same. But no, she smiles at herself, here I am, making my presence felt, in the shop window at least, the silver kilt pin winking in the window's faux candlelight.

At last, the pet shop. She does a quick tally as she passes the front counter where the shop assistant is poring over a magazine. *Fifteen* cages now. My goodness. Predictable kittens, predictable puppies. Some hamsters. Rabbits. She's never seen miniature chinchilla rabbits before, must look at them carefully. Five cages of rats seem rather a lot. They don't look much different from the wild kind. Dun-coloured mostly. A couple of sleek black ones. White ones, or are they just larger than average white mice? No. White mice are small, demure and pink-eyed. These white rats are altogether bigger. Longer in the body, more athletic; their bright eyes suggest they're more intelligent.

'Hello, Debra.'

'Hello, Ian. What are you buying then? Flea treatment? Not for your Jock, surely? He's the cleanest Scottie I've ever seen. Pattie takes him to that shampooing place on the highway, doesn't she? No, no, I don't have any pets, not since Tiger went. Nice to look, though, isn't it? I'll never get another cat. Awful to think you might die before them. How old is your Jock now? Ten? Well, you're all right then. He'll die before you, knock wood. Give my love to Pattie, and Jock too, of course.'

The birdcages have cockatiels with pink cheeks like old ladies, over-rouged. I'm one of them now, she thinks, well, not a cockatiel, but I never wear rouge these days. Not ever. A swipe of lipstick is enough. It can always double as rouge if I'm desperate for facial colour.

Years ago a woman at work saw her dabbing some lipstick on her cheeks and she sneered. 'Can't you afford blush?' Nasty bitch. It had made her feel tarty somehow, and she'd stopped dabbing at her face with cosmetics after that, in public anyway.

The budgerigars chirrup and chat. Birds of international popularity, that lot. Is there anywhere that budgies haven't been? They're probably in war zones as we speak. I'll bet they're cheaper than canaries for the mines. Cheering up prisoners in places like Alcatraz. Keeping lonely old gentlemen company. A little blue boy cocks his head to one side. 'That's right, isn't it, Buster? You're all over the world.'

Gouldian finches flit nervously across their cage. A sullen and silent sulphur-crested cockatoo turns its back on her. She stops in front of its cage. 'Who's a grumpy boy?' Nothing. 'What's up then? Cat got your tongue?' That baleful look, the yellow crest rising. Oh dear. Move on, Debra. You know when you're not wanted.

The corella in the next cage is much more entertaining. 'Hello, cocky.' The bird's mouth moves. His eyes blink and his head swings from one side to the other. He says, 'Who the fuck are you?' in a rasping voice, like a heavy smoker, choking. Debra steps back from the cage.

'What did you say?' she touches her cheek as though someone has just slapped it.

'Fuck off,' the bird says.

'Goodness me. You're a bad, bad bird.' The corella turns in circles on his perch, his beak open to expose an enamelled grey tongue. He is leering at her. Mocking. The pet shop starts to swirl.

'Excuse me. Excuse me! Please. The sign.'

Debra looks over to where the shop assistant is pointing. *Please do not speak to the parrots, especially if small children are in the shop.*

'Oh dear. Righto,' she calls, but as soon as the shop assistant is looking the other way she puts her face close to the corella's cage and whispers, 'Don't you ever speak to me like that again, you mangy shit.' The bird turns away.

'Can I help you with anything?'

She hasn't heard the shop assistant walk over to the cages. She straightens guiltily. The girl has her hands on her hips, a look of accusation on her face.

'Who taught the parrot to talk like that?' Debra asks. 'Did he teach himself or did he once belong to a sailor?' The girl gives her an odd look and Debra starts to explain that when she was little, sailors were notorious for their salty language.

The girl shrugs. 'I don't know but the sign is there to be observed. We've had a lot of complaints. Please don't talk to him.' To emphasise her point the girl gives the cage a little push. The corella's water slops and the bird hops to the other end of the perch. Debra looks around the shop. Not a child in sight. The corella has taken courage again. It hops back towards them and raises a claw to its mouth. Says, 'Give me a bloody biscuit.' The shop assistant ignores him.

Debra turns to a wall of aquariums where fish swim in languorous circles. Prosaic goldfish are being outclassed by the tropical brilliance of the fish in the next tank, where neon tetras are flashing their rainbow scales.

'Are you sure I can't help you with anything?' the shop assistant says.

Debra shakes her head. 'I'm just looking for the moment but I might buy a fish.' The girl hovers while Debra walks over to the glass. The backlit aquariums are a living, silent wall. She might be under the sea.

'My,' Debra says, turning to face the girl. 'They're pretty, aren't they? A tank like this in your lounge room would be better than watching TV.'

When at last the girl heads back to the counter, Debra stands very still until she feels transparent. She watches the goldfish, like little orange buses going about their business. She's never had much luck with goldfish. Over the years she must have flushed dozens of them down the toilet. Healthy one day, bloated, floating the next – what a waste of money. Bubbles rise from a little porcelain man in a deep-sea diving suit. A treasure chest opens and closes its porcelain lid. The tetras swim in and out of the bubbles. A couple of them play hide-and-seek amongst the weeds.

She always comes to the pet shop when she's at the mall. She's lost count of the number of times she's stood looking at the animals. The shop assistants change as regularly as the pets. Schoolkids mostly, on vacation jobs, some of them quite odd. She doesn't take too much notice of them. It's the animals she comes to see. She likes other shops in the mall, of course – the two-dollar shop and Aldi, with its tins and jars from countries she's never heard of and tables of odds and sods down the centre aisle. Freedom makes her feel, well…free…and at Michel's French cake shop, with that jaunty young cook with the handlebar moustache, she imagines herself in Paris. She's never been there either, but she's seen it plenty of times in films and on TV. The pet shop is her favourite, though. You can always find something furry or feathered with whom to while away half an hour.

She walks back to the rats and peers into their cages. They have glass sides so you can see what the rats get up to under the surface gravel and wood shavings. A rat has dug a hole and is sleeping in it, its tiny pink toes curled. The shavings are speckled with rat poo. She looks accusingly towards the front counter. The girl should clean the cages, not read a magazine. Debra taps gently on the glass but the rats don't wake up. She could spend her days like that too if she let herself. Stay in bed until lunchtime. Watch a bit of television while she eats her lunch. Have an afternoon nap. Thank goodness she's not that way inclined. Every morning at seven she's up and dressed. A brisk walk to the mall. A good long roam around the shops. Some lunch in the international food hall or Michel's. The pet shop is always the highlight. Always. The kittens, the puppies, the fish, the mice; they see her when she's peering through the glass at them. She likes that. She likes the hopeful ways the kittens come over and pat at her hands through the glass. They could be asking her to take them home. She always shakes her head and tries to explain that she's too old now to take on the responsibility. And the vet's fees. Good Lord. Those costs don't bear thinking about.

A large black rat is by itself in a cage. It's probably a male, quarantined in case it wants to start mating with the female rats. There would be a rat explosion if that were allowed. Imagine buying a rat and taking it home and then suddenly having a litter of little ones. Some child's mother would not be amused. 'Rats. They fought the dogs and killed the cats and bit the babies in their cradles.' Where's that come from? School, of course, a long time ago. *Her* poor mother hated animals. She hated lots of things, really. Still, she had plenty of reasons for being unhappy. She's forgiven her mother all of them but not the lack of pets. That's what she wanted. Always. A pet.

No, think about your parents when they were young and fresh, Debra, planning more children as soon as the war was over. They were lovely; she knows this from their photos. Her father was a rat once. Killed in Tobruk all those years ago. Ha. She hasn't made that connection until now. It must explain something. *The Rats of Tobruk*. She used to be proud to say it. 'My father was a Rat of Tobruk. Killed in 1941. He's buried over there. He was twenty-eight and I was just three when it happened.'

This rat is sleek and long of body. Pink feet and hands, a long, thick pink tail. The colour makes her think of her boyfriend's penis the first time she ever had sex. Well, the only time, really. She hadn't enjoyed it much. Afterwards she'd thought she was pregnant. Thank goodness she wasn't. Imagine the scandal if she had been. Her mother would never have forgiven her. War changes so much. It certainly changed her mother. She never remarried. She worried all the time. She'd never have forgiven Debra if she'd had a baby out of wedlock. Imagine the shame. She'd done her mother proud, though, a job in the public service, promotion, a good salary. She'd never married so wasn't affected by the marriage bar. Looked after her mother. No nursing home for her. She made sure her mother wanted for nothing but she got herself a cat as soon as she died.

'Hello, boy.'

The rat stands on its back legs, its tiny gonads visible. She is shocked with herself, her eyes drawn so quickly to them. The rat looks at her, leaning down, her face close to the glass, rat face just inches away on the other side. There weren't any boyfriends after a while; none good enough for her mother, she supposed. Certainly none good enough for her, either. Behind her she hears the corella muttering low swear words. The rat seems to be saying something in reply.

'You can see me, can't you?' she says. 'Can you hear me?' The rat's whiskers twitch. Its body stretches higher.

Debra glances quickly towards the shop assistant. The girl's head is bent low over the page. Debra stretches and carefully shifts the sheet of glass on the top of the cage. She wants to touch the rat's satin pelt. As the glass moves the full scent of the rat hits her, acrid with urine and rat sweat, a foul, oily smell. She steps back from the stink. The rat is still standing on its hind legs. It watches as Debra turns and rushes away, the rat stink in her nostrils and her mouth. The shop assistant looks up, says something as Debra hurries past.

Debra can't open her mouth, can't breathe. She is full of the rat; she can taste him on her tongue and feel the smell of him in her hair and on her skin. She passes a woman who looks familiar, who calls, 'Hello, Debra,' but Debra doesn't stop until she is outside in the sun.

A waterwheel turns slowly beside a big round pond. This is the bus stop where people come and go from the mall to the station. Debra finds an empty bench and sits for a while. She can breathe now, though the air still tastes stale. How did the rat get inside her like that? She can taste his urine, the sweaty pink moistness of his tiny feet. Behind her the mall's tinkling music tumbles out each time the electronic doors open and close. Some women laden with shopping bags laugh as they flag down a taxi. Debra sits on for a while, taking deep breaths, hoping she doesn't look odd as she huffs and puffs on an ancient wooden seat: an old woman in a tartan skirt, a rat inside her.

Debra walks home slowly, the taste of the rat diminishing as she puts some distance between herself and the mall. She will dream of animals tonight, she expects – angry foul-mouthed birds and dead goldfish and pregnant white mice and evil black rats. She gargles and cleans her teeth, changes her skirt for an old cotton housedress. She is hungry and she makes herself a large meal. It is only after she's eaten it that she regrets the missed lunch at Michel's.

By the time she goes to bed the rat is gone. Despite her anxiety about nightmare animals it is her father she dreams of, a handsome young man in a sand-coloured uniform. She calls to him through a dust storm, asks him if he'll bring her back a present from the war. She calls and calls. He must hear her because he turns, but the desert dust is swirling, the wind whipping it about. He can't see her; she is invisible to him.

'Daddy,' she shouts. 'It's me, Debbie.' And through the sand he raises his hands to blind eyes.

Salt

'Come on, Lily, hurry up.' She takes the child's hand in hers. They choose the upstairs gangplank, a steep ramp to the upper deck. Lily looks around as they climb, at the green-and-yellow bulk of the ferry, the iron railings with their polished wooden balustrades, the slatted seats. The ferry is called *Freshwater*.

People push from behind, wanting a seat on deck. A man comments on Dorrie's scarf. She is used to it. She ignores him and quickly finds two spaces and claims them. She pulls her niece close to her. 'Aah,' Dorrie says as she sits down, ignoring the curious glances of the other passengers. She presses her back to the hard wooden seat and lifts her face to the sun, feeling the caress of a breeze, salt in it, crystalline and heavy like a sprinkle of rock salt on fish and chips. Just the thought of food makes her mouth water. Batter puffed and golden, potato scallops, the soft, steaming white potato inside its crisp batter shell. Squat fingers of chips. White fish with a shadow of grey skin still on it. Vinegar as it hits the hot batter. And salt, lots and lots of salt.

'Aunty Dorrie?'

'Yes, pet.'

'Can I stand down there?' The child points down the rail to where a space has opened up.

She will be able to see her from here. 'Of course you can, sweetie, but no further. Okay?'

The child skips off and Dorrie closes her eyes again. Fish and chips. And afterwards? Really good vanilla ice-cream in one of those pale orange cones that taste of nothing much. Her local milk bar used to have a vanilla cone above the door, a big plastic one that was lit up at night from a light bulb within. She always bought her ice-cream from there because she loved to watch the owner take a cone from a silver dispenser, a silver ice-cream scoop from a water-filled tin. A childhood of rituals, of food that's never tasted as good since: liquorice allsorts, fairy floss, hamburgers with fried onions and iceberg lettuce, a melted slice of cheese, beetroot. A proper hamburger roll, one with a shiny hard top and a soft white inside. Not like the cottonwool rolls kids eat their hamburgers in today. Cream buns, cream horns, horseshoe rolls, pineapple crush drinks with bits of pineapple that got stuck in the drinking straw, friends' birthday parties with cocktail frankfurts dipped in tomato sauce. Fairy bread and lime jelly crystal sandwiches.

She hasn't thought about food like this for ages. Circular Quay smells of fried food, that's what's done it: that Italian place with its tables and umbrellas, the cafes on all the wharves, their food scents competing with one another. She glances towards Lily. She's leaning over the rail looking at the water. Standing on her toes, her dress has ridden up, exposing her knickers. Dorrie looks at the other people at the rails to check none of them are perving on the girl. You can't be too careful these days. You can't trust anyone, not schoolteachers or actors or priests.

The ferry is full. A bell rings on the wharf and some stragglers start to run. A man further up the wharf whistles and a wire gate closes. The stragglers make it to the gang-plank. They're on board now, laughing, puffed out with their exertion. The gangplank is raised, slowly, a bell still ringing. Lily looks back at her, awe on her face. Dorrie nods, and says, 'It's good, isn't it?' The child can't possibly have heard her over the din of bells and revving ferry engines and the mechanical elevation of the gangplank, but she nods and smiles and leans forward again, looking down at the water churning now as the ferry moves away from the wharf. I should have included cake on my list, Dorrie thinks. Really light passionfruit sponges with cream in the middle, finger buns with pink icing and lots of butter, fruit-cake, neenish tarts, homemade lamingtons bristling with shredded coconut.

The ferry heads up the harbour, past the posh apartments with palm trees in front of them, past the Opera House. The quay has changed so much since she was a little girl, no Opera House then, just its foundations and the oddly shaped shells unfurling under scaffolding and controversy. Everyone had an opinion about the design. Some liked it, some didn't. It was too grand for plain folks like us. Well, they're eating their words now.

All the tourists move to the rails to take a photo of the white sails, and for a moment Lily is obscured by a tall German man who says, '*Ein foto, mein liebling.*' He gives directions loudly to his wife, motions for her to stand against the rails with the Opera House behind her. She says, '*Nein, Heinrich, genug.*' Dorrie smiles. Photo fatigue. She sees it every time she gets a ferry over to Manly. She remembers feeling it herself as a kid. Her father was always making her and her sister Lynette pose, the sun in their eyes, so in every photo they were squinting. 'You look like a Chinaman, Dorrie,' he'd shout. 'Smile properly, look up.' When the photos came back from processing, her eyes sun-slits, head cocked awkwardly to one side, he'd cluck his tongue. 'Told you.' And he'd recite some inane and awful verse about Chinamen and where they hid their money.

What was her mother doing during all those trips? Fussing. Checking her purse for keys, for money, hankies, hair clips. Did her mother ever have a day out where she wasn't the self-nominated worrier? Probably not. They had good times, though, Manly always being a family favourite, places on Botany Bay too, like Dolls Point or Ramsgate. A picnic basket, some corned beef sandwiches, fruit, an ice-cream cone before heading home if she and Lynette had behaved themselves.

The ferry is on the open harbour now, moving in a stately way past inlets and bays, pale houses that hug the hills, a fuzz of gum trees, the purple of jacarandas. Yachts, little boats. The people on the ferry wave to them and sometimes the people on the boats wave back. Sydney never felt as opulent back then, not like now. People have to show off their wealth now. It would have been considered vulgar when she was little. If you had a lot of money you kept it to yourself, stayed with your own kind in suburbs like the ones the ferry is passing, didn't try to make out there was something wrong with you if you were down on your luck.

She looks around, wondering how many of the people on the ferry have been through hard times. Bit hard to tell with tourists. They all wear a kind of uniform: casual clothes, sensible walking shoes, little backpacks, cloth hats. As for the locals, well, they're dressed pretty much the same. Not like when she was a kid and they'd have to wear their Sunday best on outings. God, how she hated the stiff frocks and net petticoats and little hats her mother sometimes made them wear. She'd look with envy at the other kids in shorts and muu-muus and jeans. 'Why can't we dress like *them*?'

'Because you just *can't*, Dorothy, now sit still.'

'Aunty Dorrie?' Lily is standing in front of her. 'Can I have an iceblock?' Other children are eating ices and sweets. The ferry has a kiosk.

'No, pet, wait till you get to Manly. We'll have fish and chips and an ice-cream from one of those really posh ice-cream places with lots and lots of flavours. Much nicer.'

Lily seems unconvinced but she walks slowly back to her spot on the rails and pushes her way between the two German tourists. Dorrie stands and leans on the rails too. They are nearing the Heads now and she always loves the ferry's sway and roll when it hits the currents. She whispers the words, *the Heads* – that yawning gap between north and south headlands, a mythical space through which you enter or leave Sydney. How many times, as a kid, had she heard someone say, 'God, it was rough as we crossed the Heads.' So she always approaches this part of the trip with anticipation and a fear that rarely lives up to its promise. Today's harbour is more a kitten than a tiger. It offers a little swell and roll, nothing too dramatic, as the ferry moves towards the tame opulence of Fairy Bower and then Manly wharf.

The railing is hot as Dorrie leans against it, the iron thick with paint and layers of rust, little salt crystals gritty under her fingers. She turns her back to the water and looks at the passengers. Families, largely, grandparents, aunties and great-aunties like herself. A man in a suit is standing alone at the prow, watching closely where the ferry is heading. A 'darkie', her father would have said. She can't help but remember his words even though she would never use them. Words hurt; she's learned that surely enough.

With a quick glance back at Lily she walks towards the prow. 'Ooh,' someone shouts as the ferry rolls suddenly and water splashes onto the deck below. More people have stood and they look towards the sea, the two Heads, south and north, like the lion's paws of very big sphinxes.

'It's always choppy here,' she says to the man.

He turns towards her. 'Big waves?'

'Sometimes they come right over here.' She points to the prow. 'Mind you, that's once in a blue moon.'

He seems to be enjoying the pitch and roll too. The ferry is solid under their feet, the deck timbers bleached and salty. More water splashes onto the lower deck, more people squeal and laugh.

'You a tourist?' Dorrie asks.

'No,' he says. 'I live here.'

She says, 'Well, you've picked a nice place to settle, that's for sure.' She glances towards Lily. The child seems to have forgotten all about ices and sweets. Dorrie can see what's left of the old Manly fun pier up ahead. Not much of it remains. Not the merry-go-round, not the helter skelter. 'Where are you from originally, then?'

He must be used to the question. He sighs, smiles coolly. 'In Australia?' There is a hint of mockery in his tone that she doesn't like at first, then she hears her schoolteacher's voice. 'Don't ask people personal questions. Don't ask what they earn or what things cost. You certainly shouldn't ask new Australians where they came from. After a war, the last thing they want is to be reminded of what they've been through.'

'Look.' Lily is grinning at them. She holds out her palm, a twenty-cent piece on it.

'Who gave you that?' Dorrie snaps.

Lily looks towards the rail, to the Germans who are snapping photos again. 'That lady.'

Dorrie's voice is hoarse as she says, 'I've told you never to take money from strangers, Lily.'

The man reaches down and examines the coin. 'Twenty cents. That's a platypus.' When Lily looks puzzled, he holds the coin up. 'Every Australian coin has an animal. Ten cents is a lyrebird. Five cents is an echidna.'

He passes the coin to Dorrie. 'I'll mind it for you, Lil,' she says. 'Don't go far now. We're just about there.'

People are standing and picking up their things. From the other side of the ferry she hears the bell and the mechanical lowering of the gangplank. 'I'd better get going.'

Softening, he says, 'It is all right to ask me where I am from. I am used to it and I am not ashamed.'

Dorrie lifts her hand to her head, adjusts her scarf. The sun is hot against it. She has wound it on too tightly today. She nods. When she was little there were lots of old pink countries on maps. Lots of new ones now, lots of fighting between different people.

He looks at her head, at the scarf. It's lopsided, she's sure. 'What has happened to you? You are ill?'

Dorrie nods. 'Well, I have been.'

She looks down at the water – so clear, so turquoise – drawing pleasure from its intense blue-green. Everything feels more urgent these days. Everything must be collected and gleaned and shared. No memory pushed aside, no pleasure deferred. Like telling her niece about her childhood trips to Manly, and embarking the ferry through the frightening wooden turnstiles at Circular Quay. Like Manly's amusement pier and old-fashioned tearooms, the picnics under the Norfolk pines with her family. When being tumbled over and over by a too-boisterous wave, her father laughing fit to burst on the shore, seemed the most terrifying thing that could ever happen to you. She smells everything more intensely now too. Salt again, and the blue, fishy smell of the water. There is fried food and perfume and the crisp ironed smell of the man's neat white shirt. She looks down at Lily's hair, the parting exposing the child's pale skull. If she lowered her face to it, Lily's hair would smell of apples, that shampoo Lily's mother uses, a luminous emerald green in a long plastic bottle.

'I got the all clear last week but it'll take a bit of time for my hair to come back. My appetite's raging, though. I could eat a horse and chase the jockey as my father used to say.'

When the man looks puzzled she explains, 'It's an old Aussie term for being so hungry you'd eat anything.'

'Oh,' he says. 'I have known such hunger.'

Lily is standing beside her now, holding tight to her hand. She watches the man shyly.

'And this is our little celebration, isn't it, Lil? Our special day at the beach.'

At four, after she and Lily have walked to the ocean side of Manly, explored the market, played on the sand, she buys some fish and chips and they settle on the promenade to eat them. The seagulls rage in the air above. The breeze tears at the fish and chip paper. There's not enough salt or brown malt vinegar. Something is missing – her childhood, she supposes.

On the way back to the ferry she buys them both an ice-cream, chocolate for Lily, vanilla for herself. The evening ferry is nowhere near as crowded and she finds herself looking for the man she'd chatted to earlier. Lily is asleep by the time the ferry turns into Circular Quay. Should she wake her? The sky has darkened and the lights are on in all the buildings. She checks to make sure no one is looking and takes off the scarf and gives her head a good scratch. As soon as Lily is properly awake she'll tell her about the neon phoenix that used to rise off one of the sandstone buildings down here near the water.

They always looked forward to it as they entered the quay, tired, happy – her mother, her father, Lynette. A bird, rising from flames and flying up and up and up.

'Wake up, sweetie,' Dorrie says. 'I'm hungry again. Are you?'

Some People's Lives

Every weekday Willem van de Pol catches the 7.15 from Kings Cross to Penrith, taking a slow walk up Elizabeth Bay Road to the station, stepping carefully over his memories of the street along the way. He passes the site of the Townhouse Hotel, where as a starstruck younger man, he'd sat in the foyer waiting for someone famous to appear, a singer, an actor or comedian, their faces familiar from the TV. The Cross was full of Hungarians and Poles and Russians in those days, even a few Dutch like himself. It wasn't unusual to walk from one end of Darlinghurst Road to the other without hearing a word of English. Despite the united nations of the streets it had all seemed so vividly Australian, the light especially, everything sharp-edged. When he saw his first Jeffrey Smart painting he at last understood. The place was so bright and brutal and empty – thankless – though Willem could never say that to his father, so thankful was he that they were all safely here.

As soon as they'd arrived in Sydney his father had taken over the lease on a bookshop in Macleay Street. He thought he'd make a killing amongst an educated elite of Europeans, just as his forebears had done in Rotterdam. But too many of the people in the Cross were running away. Willem had once seen a dog just like them, running, searching for what God only knew. Migrants spent more time in the Cross's dimly lit coffee bars staring into their cups than at the pages of a book. Despite this, the bookshop had done well enough for a while. Willem and his sister Jopie had helped out, stocking up on the paperbacks favoured by the Cross's growing population of young bohemians. But no matter how much Willem tried to convince him otherwise, his father preferred to buy leather-bound classics, some ordered especially in a customer's old language. The Magyars and Viennese and Russians and Poles might pull themselves slowly away from an afternoon of quiet coffee drinking, might even want to reacquaint themselves with a lost culture. 'Look, Tolstoy,' his father would say, patting a blue-covered volume. Ibsen, Goethe, Hugo, Turgenev. Slowly Willem had learned to love those writers too.

Jopie, pale as candlelight, her silvery hair wound round and round in knots at the nape of her neck, which reminded Willem of a horse's droppings. Jopie, the drawcard for lonely men and randy bohemians. She'd taken to wearing beatnik clothes in her teens – black poloneck sweaters and tight black matador pants and little flat ballet shoes, their father sniffing his disapproval as she climbed up and down the shop's ladder, some mesmerised customer waiting below, politely holding the ladder steady in case she fell. Who's she trying to fool? She's as agile as a cat, Willem thought, watching his sister dance up and down.

Every Friday night they closed the shop an hour early and walked back to their flat together. A snippet of the Harbour Bridge was visible from the sitting room, their table set brightly with white linen and candles on stems and noodle soup and chicken with herbs and grilled fish Rotterdam style and apple cake with lashings of cream. The wine they drank was imported because his father could never trust local wines with names like Flying Duck or Blue Nun or Porphyry Pearl, so he bought instead from the Italian merchants in Surry Hills and carried the bottles home in a creaking shopping trolley two dozen at a time. Willem's mother in a starched white apron saying, '*Vooruit, eet je bordje leeg*,' eat your dinner, her husband cajoling her to speak English, her hand fluttering from plate to plate – enough food for her extended family too if any of them had survived the war.

Under the plane trees the Cross's garbage bins are over-flowing with the rubbish of the night before, with fried food containers and polystyrene cups. Mindful of his freshly polished shoes, Willem steps around them. His parents have been dead for twenty years, his father first, his mother close to follow. Jopie married Shaun, a university lecturer, and moved to Melbourne to raise three sons. They agreed to sell the family flat soon after their mother had died. With Jopie gone it was far too big for Willem anyway. He bought a smaller place in Elizabeth Bay Road, just one bedroom and a study with a lovely view of Rushcutters Bay. He sold off his parents' heavy furniture – too much in the style of Biedermeier to make much money at auction but enough to replace it with something more contemporary, more in keeping with his new apartment's light, the shimmer of water that often took his ceiling by surprise, the birdsong that effervesced upwards from the park's trees. Light and modern, his only concession to the past was a set of his father's old leather-bound books.

People rush into Kings Cross station. They'll get out at Town Hall or Martin Place, Willem knows, so he doesn't mind being crammed into the train. He'll have a seat from Central to Penrith and some quiet time to look out of the train window at the inner suburbs. Little terrace houses. Little back gardens. Graffiti. The ugly arse of the city, its soot-grimed sidings and crisscrossing electric wires.

'Willem.'

He turns towards the voice. A woman pushes her way to him. It's Rita Keys from the flat below his.

'Hello,' says Willem. 'You're up early today.'

'A teacher is ill. I'm filling in.'

He remembers, then, a story she'd told him at their apartment building's Christmas party. Rita has given up full-time work but likes to do the odd stint of relief teaching. All said over a platter of dolmades, sleek as otters, glistening with oil.

Navy blue suit, her hair done in a different, more business-like style. 'You look nice,' Willem says. 'Very elegant.'

Rita touches her hair, smiles.

Now the carriage is empty Willem moves to a newly vacated seat and Rita sits down beside him. She seems to sense that he wants to think, so she silently fiddles with the clasp of her bag. Stanmore. Petersham. Ashfield. Croydon.

Then she says, 'I'm having a party next Saturday if you'd like to come.'

Willem turns to regard her. Through the window behind he sees an old building smothered in bougainvillea. What colour is that? Something between orange and pink, so bright it seems to burn the air around it.

'A party? Yes. That would be nice.'

'Eight o'clock.' Burwood. She stands. 'My school is halfway between Burwood and Strathfield,' she says. 'It's a lovely walk from the station.'

Alone again, Willem settles back to enjoy the train, to look around at the other passengers now the carriage is almost empty. He saw a young man on the train a few months ago, florid, shouting at the other passengers. Cajoling, laughing all the way from Central, where he'd been talking to a group of men on the platform one minute, and on the train the next. The men looked bemused as he waved at them from the door. Laughed uncomfortably as he called out their names. Once seated he'd begun a conversation with himself. He'd shouted for a while, then he'd moved closer to Willem, and Willem had been very careful not to catch his eye. Curious, though, he'd glanced across at the man anyway, chatting to no one in particular about whatever the train passed. The railway yards at Eveleigh, children in pale blue uniforms pouring into a school, Rookwood cemetery, the graves overgrown with lantana. The mosque at Auburn.

Trains full of crazy people. On one of his first trips into Sydney's suburbs, such a long time ago now, Willem had seen an old man carefully unwrap a half-pound packet of butter, peeling the waxy paper clear of the yellow log. Then he'd eaten it in small careful bites. Who would eat butter like this? Still, Willem's mouth had begun to moisten as he watched the masticatory care the man took, bite by bite. The train had pulled into Wollstonecraft and Willem got out. He'd never picked up a slab of butter since without thinking of that man.

Willem checks his notebook for the day's appointments. Meetings, of course: academics spent more time in meetings now than anything else. While he has the diary out he checks the date of Rita's party. Nothing on that night. He'll go for a little while. He's been spending too much time alone lately. It's easy to close the door at night and shut the world out. The long train trip back into the city, the train filling with passengers in reverse: Blacktown, Parramatta, Lidcombe, Strathfield, Burwood. Pushing his way across the crowded platform at Town Hall, then the Cross again and the slow walk home along Elizabeth Bay Road. On balmy nights he often feels the terrible tension between wanting to stay out and wanting to get back to his books and music and his solitary dinner: agoraphobia, the fear of the marketplace, the pull of the social world struggling with the pull of retreat. This is especially the case on nights when the twilight descends slowly, like someone languidly closing heavy-lidded eyes, the trees in Macleay Street atwitter with sparrows, the sky washed pink. In Europe he'd choose an outdoor cafe and order an aperitif. He'd stay on for dinner, share a bottle of wine with friends. There are no friends now, not people he'd want to spend his evenings with, anyway, just work colleagues, that polite name for people with whom economic necessity forces you to spend your days.

Willem sees Rita on the train again the next morning but the crush is so great he can only dip his head towards her in greeting. When the crowd disperses he sees she has a place on one of the seats that face each other across the carriage. He prefers to face the direction the train is going, so he moves away from her and sits by himself. When the train reaches Burwood she taps lightly on his window and gives a little wave. He waves in return as the train moves along the platform, then he settles back to look around at the other passengers. His briefcase holds half-a-dozen student papers. He thinks about marking them but the train has its own particular allure, a non-space, a non-time, in which to reflect about his life, past and present, and to watch the way other people live theirs. Some mornings he likes to play a particular game. He chooses a house, any house, and imagines living in it. It might be one of the inner-city terraces that back down to the railway line at Newtown or one of Stanmore's imposing mansions, or a postwar fibro house in Blacktown. He imagines a wife and some children, a cat, a dog, a station wagon. His father once said a man could only call himself successful if he'd planted a tree, written a book, fathered a child. He's done only one of these things. He's written five books; of that he is very proud, but there is no time left for children now. As for the tree – he looks at the houses and their fantasy lives, and he sees himself planting one of the purple trees that are so popular in the suburbs: jacaranda, tibouchina. Even saying the words makes him yearn for Saturday afternoons in the local plant nursery, pushing a shopping trolley beside a wife and arguing about which border plants to buy.

That evening Willem changes his walk home. Instead of leaving Kings Cross station by his usual route he goes down the hill towards Rushcutters Bay and cuts across the park. A low wall follows the water line, on the right towards the grand houses of Darling Point, on the left towards Elizabeth Bay and the Cross. He takes the path on the left. The streets rise sharply from the water and he stretches his head back to look for his building. There it is, sandwiched between other apartment blocks, a messy conglomeration of prewar red-brick buildings and the glass boxes that have grown beside them over the past few decades. He counts upwards and across till he finds his window. In the twilight's trickery he sees himself at his desk at the window, his books piled up on the desktop, his papers illuminated by his reading lamp. He sees his body leaning backwards in his chair, tilting it till his feet can rest on the desk. He's looking out at the green fuse of Rushcutters Bay Park, the water emerald, the sky darkening. Willem looks at Willem bound to his desk, as doomed as Prometheus on his rock. Willem inside reaches for another book, another essay to mark, another article to write. His life will pass tethered to his papers, each sunny day spent indoors, each weekend spent catching up on work.

The falling sun dances on the water. The perfumed twilight settles around him. He leans against the stone wall and sees the water brush against it. He is hungry for the sensation of water and grass on skin.

Saturday night and it is time to go to Rita's party. Willem can hear people coming up the stairs, calling greetings to one another. Music is rising through his floor. He can feel it through the soles of his shoes. A knock on Rita's door, the music and voices of her flat louder as the door opens, Rita's voice all smiles and greetings. 'Come in, come in.'

He's eaten some eggs on toast. He's finished marking the last of his students' essays. He's watched the *ABC News* and waited so he can arrive at the party not too early, leave not too late if he finds no one to talk to. In front of the mirror he looks long and hard at his face. It has grown into his father's, he sees, the flat cheeks, the family dimple in the chin, the fair hair now almost white. His shirt looks freshly pressed. He won't add a tie. It's three years since he's had sex with a woman. Three years since he kissed a woman passionately on the lips. Will the party offer a break in the drought? He smiles slowly at the thought and the face in the mirror smiles back, but there is something haunting in the way the smile bares the teeth, something mean and pathetic. He goes back to the lounge room and puts on a record. Brahms's double concerto, Bernard Haitink, a fellow Dutchman, conducting. More voices on the stairs, Rita's door closing and opening. He listens to the people, to the music. He will not go to the party.

On Monday morning Willem walks slowly up Elizabeth Bay Road. He is early and will take an earlier train. He has passed Rita's recycle bin, the empty wine bottles relaying social triumph outside her apartment door. The train is crowded and he is pushed hard against the other commuters and the warm companionship of their bodies. He has a lecture at ten, a meeting from twelve till two. So much work, he thinks, making his way at last to an empty seat.

Drones

As Terry waits for his cheese on toast to grill he leans over to the kitchen's open window. The sharp edge of the kitchen bench presses into his stomach and the night air comes forward to greet him. In its chill and dewy softness he can smell the flowering jasmine that has covered the old outdoor toilet. Its flowers are just visible, white starbursts in the velvety dark. Frogs are calling shrilly in his neighbour's pond – sweet, girly, high-pitched green frogs, low-growling bullfrogs. The pond is full of yellow water iris. Terry saw the bright, scrolled flowers when the old man called him over to the fence this afternoon to present him with a bowl of homegrown tomatoes.

When the cheese is bubbling and golden, Terry takes a stubby of beer from the fridge and goes into the lounge room. He raises his plate towards Nicki, who is sprawled on the couch.

'Sure you don't want one?'

Nicki glances towards the toast, then back to the TV. 'No thanks.'

Terry looks at the screen too. He can't read the subtitles very well from here. SBS should put a black band along the bottom of the screen so the white writing stands out. He walks forward and squints. A man is talking about the death of his wife and kids.

'Why do you always watch these gloomy shows on TV?'

'What?'

'SBS. All these foreign films with unhappy endings.' He sits down and Nicki shuffles up the couch a bit, until she's resting heavily against his ribs. She reaches across and takes his sandwich and bites off a piece, then she holds her hand out for the stubby and drinks some beer.

She chews and drinks and says, 'I don't.'

Terry puts the plate and the stubby out of her reach. 'Yes, you do.'

'What do you want to watch – the sport?'

'No, but there has to be something cheerier than this.'

'It's gritty realism.'

'What, kids getting blown up?'

'It happens. You saw the Gaza news coverage.'

'Yes, but that was the news.'

'Well, people make films about wars too.'

An advertisement comes on and Nicki goes to the bathroom. While she's out of the room Terry takes the remote control and flicks through the channels. The ABC has a documentary about the Great Barrier Reef and he looks at the exhilarating beauty of the water, so clear you can see the white sand below the surface. He wants to take Nicki up there for a holiday. His mates reckon Dunk Island is the best. It has lots of bars and partying, good pools and little bays to snorkel in.

Nicki is back. She sits down and takes the remote control from him. She puts the SBS film on. Some little boys and girls are hiding from the Taliban, or are they American soldiers? Terry can't make out the writing. 'Are they goodies or baddies?' he asks.

'It's a bit more ambiguous than that.'

Ambiguous has become one of Nicki's favourite words. Terry blames it on her university course. She's been using bigger words since she started an MA in journalism. She watches SBS a lot too, for a more balanced view of the world, she says.

'Can't we just watch something lifestyle for a change?'

'I thought you hated reality TV. You said it was like a cancer on our screens,' Nicki replies. 'You said it's just advertising for supermarkets and building firms and furniture stores.'

'Well, yes, it is.'

'So why watch it?'

'For escapism? At least it's happy.'

Nicki snorts. 'It's not happy. The people on those shows are competitive and they're really rude. It's all about rushing to finish things or "go home" if you fail. And the judges are up themselves.'

'So?'

'So, it makes people think that there's something wrong with them if they don't have a gorgeous house or can't cook like a Michelin-starred chef.'

Terry looks around the lounge room. Not even he and Nicki are immune to reality TV's pervasiveness. They'd decided on their dark orange feature wall after seeing one just like it on a renovation special. Nicki got the idea for their milk-crate bookshelves in a *Home Beautiful* magazine.

'Well, let's watch a cooking show then.'

'Cooking? You hate those shows too.'

'No, I don't. You get great ideas from them, like the way they spread the sauce across the plate so it looks nice under the meat.'

'Yeah, I can just see you doing that.'

'I might.'

Explosions and screams; a child is begging. Terry looks the other way. He can't help it. This kid is going to cop it if he doesn't just run off. The tension is awful. Thank God, the kid's had the good sense to head towards some palm trees. Terry takes another bite of his sandwich. The melted cheese has solidified into something resembling glue. It tastes rubbery now and unpleasant against his teeth. He chews carefully. He can't stand shows where kids get hurt. Kids covered in burns or cuts or bruises – he gets up and walks away from the news when they show that. And those warnings: 'Some viewers may find the following images disturbing...' They're never enough of a warning, really, to prepare you for what's coming. All the people watching the news as they eat their dinners off their laps in front of the TV, then some mangled corpse or diseased villager or massacred kids appear in full colour on their screens. He moves his body so his outstretched legs can be raised to the coffee table. Nicki moves over to give him more room.

'Can we just watch the end of this movie? It's only another twenty minutes.'

'Those kids will get killed.'

'I know.'

'Do you want that?'

'Don't be silly, Terry. There's nothing I can do about it. It's a film. Go make us some coffee or something.'

'You won't sleep.'

'Chamomile tea, then.'

Terry wipes down the kitchen benches and runs some water over his plate. He leans back towards the open window. The frogs are silent now. The scent of jasmine is less strident. His neighbour's lights are out. The old fellow gets up early so he's usually in bed by nine. Sometimes, when he goes out in his dressing-gown to look for the morning paper, Terry sees him weeding his tomato patch. Terry has never seen a garden so tidy, both front and back given over to neat rows of staked tomatoes punctuated with the dense leafiness of basil plants. Lemon trees are pruned hard annually and fertilised with something that smells, to Terry, like human shit. Whatever he uses, the old man's garden likes it. All summer its produce is shared with the neighbourhood.

He turns back to the room, its lights sharply bright after the dark outside. The kitchen's clutter offers comfort after all the world's horrors. He looks at the mugs and plates, the mishmash of cutlery that never seems to come out of the dishwasher quite clean enough. From here he can hear the TV but not see it, and the sounds of war are softly muted, the explosions dull thuds.

He jumps when he hears a noise behind him. It's Linus, coming in through the cat flap. 'Hello, boy,' Terry says, but the cat walks straight past him and jumps up onto the couch and Nicki's lap. Terry fills the bowl with dried cat food anyway and changes his water. He looks into the laundry to check that the litter tray is clean. The kettle has boiled so he makes Nicki a mug of chamomile tea. Only then does he go back to the couch, but before he sits down he pulls a chocolate bar from his shirt pocket with a flourish.

'Chocolate? Where did you find that?'

'Never mind. I have a secret stash.'

'Good man.'

Terry doesn't tell her that he needs the comfort of it. Eating something sweet seems to override the misery on the TV. 'Why is that kid running away?' he asks between bites.

'The Americans have arrived. He's going to tell his father.'

'The terrorist guy?'

'The freedom fighter, yes.'

'I thought that was his uncle. He's the good terrorist who wants to negotiate. The others just want to blow the hell out of everything. Is that right?'

'Just watch it. Okay?'

'Shit! I told you the kid would get killed.'

Nicki takes a sip of her tea. 'He's not dead. See, he's crawling towards the gate. Now he's in the compound. Oh, thank goodness. He's made it.'

Terry leans forward to peer at the screen. 'What's that?'

'What?'

'That thing in the sky.'

'It's a drone.'

'A drone? Jesus Christ. Now what?'

'They're running out the back. See? The man has the kid over his shoulder.'

'They'll never make it.'

'Shit.'

Linus is purring loudly and kneading at Nicki's lap. She doesn't usually like that. It makes her think she's got a fat stomach. The cat only chooses her to knead, she says, because she's soft and flabby, a perfect cat cushion. The cat turns a couple of circles and settles. Nicki scratches his under-chin.

'See. I told you,' Terry snorts. 'All dead. Now it's the credits? What kind of ending is that?'

'We're meant to not know whether they get away or not. Ambiguity. We have to have hope.'

'Well, I don't have any hope. As far as I'm concerned they're dead.'

'Don't eat all the chocolate.'

'Give me the remote.'

'Why?'

'I need to watch something funny.'

'*The Footy Show*?'

'So? Why not, if it's still on. I need a laugh before I go to bed.'

They sit in the half-light while the man on TV compares the front row forwards of Souths and Easts. Nicki sips her tea. Terry sucks the last piece of chocolate. Ever since he was a little boy his capacity to make sweets last had been the envy of all his friends. He's proud of that. The chocolate is still a discernible block on his tongue.

Nicki prods him in the ribs. 'Don't make that noise.'

'What noise?'

'That horrible slurping sound with your teeth.'

'That's you, slurping the tea.'

'No, it's not – it's you. You sound like an old man sucking on his false teeth.'

'Do you really think those little kids survived?'

'Yeah. The director always does that. He's Iranian. He works from a different aesthetic. American film directors like all the loose ends tied up.'

'Listen to you.'

'What?'

He digs her in the ribs. 'I'm going to ring SBS and suggest you for *The Movie Show*.'

'Ha ha.' She chucks a cushion at him.

Their mucking around has irritated the cat. He jumps down from the couch and flees to the kitchen. Terry hears the deliberate crunch as Linus eats the dried food in his bowl, then the cat flap rises and slaps shut behind him.

When Nicki is in the shower Terry puts out the rubbish, stopping to admire his neighbour's garden again, its basil softly rustling in the breeze. A TV is droning in one of the other houses. The street slopes down to the highway and on each side of it, he can make out the bulky outlines of every house's rubbish bin, angled to the kerb to give the collectors easy access. The street trees are jacarandas and Illawarra flame trees, some councillor's decision years ago so that when the trees are in flower there's a patchwork of purple and red, red and purple, all the way down the hill. The streetlights are too bright to allow a good view of the stars. He makes a mental note to take Nicki somewhere on the weekend where they can lie down and look up at the night sky, somewhere dark and quiet, a beach or maybe the Royal National Park.

Nicki is in bed when he goes back inside. She's naked under the covers and she gives him a playful flash with the sheets.

'Woo woo.' He laughs but there isn't much humour in it. Not much desire either, though when he first saw her he felt the stirrings of an erection. Nicki has always been good at sensing his mood. Something resigned creeps up her body. She looks at the clock and says she'd better get some sleep because she has to do an office presentation in the morning. Terry nods and goes to the bathroom and cleans his teeth.

In the dark, unable to sleep, he thinks about the movie's little kids. Nicki talks about ambiguity but she's an optimist too. They'll have kids one day. They'll get on top of their mortgage and she'll be able to give up work for a while. They'll take holidays in places like Dunk Island and make love in a cabana with a straw-scented and woven roof. The sea will crash onto the sand, which will be good, because that way no one will hear when Nicki comes really loudly. There will be no more depressing films, that's for sure. No more drones, no more bombs.

Nicki snores softly and he puts his face close to hers. He kisses her and she wakes and moves towards him. As he enters her he laughs softly and she laughs back. Ambiguous. There is nothing ambiguous about this. 'Oh,' she says. 'Oh.'

On the lawn outside the cat caterwauls and the frogs croak and plop about in their neighbour's pond. Here, there are no drones, no bombs. And somewhere, beyond the deep and impenetrable dark, there are stars.

Little Kerrie

'Where do you want to go?'

Tommy's dog, Kip, is pulling against the lead, choking in a sudden, vomiting way then looking back at Tommy as if to say, 'Hurry up, *you're* doing this to me.' Kerrie looks down at her dog. Trixie is quiet and well behaved. She's placed her dog bottom neatly between the cracks in the footpath. Her lead is loose in Kerrie's hand. 'Milperra?' she says.

Kerrie has sixpence in her pocket and she hopes Tommy has sixpence in his. With that they can buy Paddle Pops, some lollies, a packet of cheese Twisties. She yanks at Trixie and the dog follows her. Kip is already pulling at his lead and Tommy is walking quickly to keep up.

Kerrie's mum is up at Auntie Jane's. She'll be there for hours getting her hair permed. Auntie Jane has become the street's cheap hairdresser. She does everyone's hair. The mothers have tightly permed flat curls, the children pudding bowls with fringes that start at their crowns and end just above their eyebrows. This is how Tommy's hair has been cut, and Kerrie's: anyone seeing them for the first time might think them brother and sister.

Kip stops to sniff, pisses, stops to sniff, pisses again. Tommy pulls hard on the lead and Kip follows, his leg still up in the air, his piss spraying. Trixie is much more ladylike. She squats when she wees. She doesn't like people watching her when she does a number two, her dog eyes go furtive and embarrassed. Kerrie always looks the other way until she's finished.

Tommy glances at the watch he started to wear a week ago. 'It's half past three already. There's no time to go to the river. Let's go to Black Charlie's Hill.'

'Okay.' Kerrie likes the walk to Black Charlie's, up and up and up. From the highest point in Edgar Street you can see the Harbour Bridge. Only just the top of it, and a long way off, but the view always excites her. Here in the suburbs the bridge seems to offer a much brighter life. White Persian cats live in the rooms at the top of the pylons, her teacher said.

Her father laughed when she told him she was moving there one day. 'Why would you want to live near the bridge, little Kerrie? Have you seen all the poky little houses we pass on the way to Sydney? Erskineville, St Peters and Redfern? The houses near the bridge are like that. We left England to get away from those sorts of terraces.'

He's built a nice new fibro house – 'a bungalow,' he calls it proudly. There are lots of houses like it on the way to Black Charlie's: new, fibro, only one or two made of brick. Kerrie's favourite has a flat and tilting roof and a wide veranda, a big wrought-iron butterfly on the front wall. Once she and her girlfriend, Gina, walked up and touched it but the owner came out and asked them what they thought they were doing. 'You're trespassing, girls,' the woman said. 'You wouldn't want me to call the police, would you?' Gina waited till they got to the corner, then she turned to the house and stuck out her tongue. Gina's father is Ukrainian and he works for the railways and he rides a bike to work. He always waves whenever he passes Kerrie, his legs short and brown and muscly as he pedals. Her dad's legs are pale and freckled.

Tommy is fiddling with his watch. Kip is straining and choking. Last week Kerrie asked Tommy where he got the watch and he said, 'Found it.' He doesn't care who sees it so it proves his parents don't mind. Tommy is always telling his parents what to do. He says, 'I want a shilling,' and he gets it. Kerrie has to wait till her mother isn't looking then she nicks from her purse. She hasn't been caught yet but she's seen the puzzled look on her mother's face when she counts out her change.

They stop at the top of Edgar Street and turn to look east. It's cloudy now and the bridge isn't visible. Tomorrow it's going to rain, Kerrie's father said. 'What else? Work all week, it's sunny. Get a day off, it rains.' Kerrie keeps looking towards the bridge, willing it to appear from behind the clouds. A long strand of light might illuminate it like the picture in Sunday school where God sent down a ray of sunshine and blinded a man on a horse.

'Come on,' Tommy calls. He's gone ahead and let Kip off his lead. Kip is running in wide circles, his tongue flapping.

Trixie watches him like the girls watch the boys in their playground. Boys are stupid. Boys are rough. Kerrie bends to let Trixie off her lead too. 'Come on, Trix,' she calls, running towards Tommy.

This is the only place where the bush has been left alone, though roads are being cut through it. Wattle trees bend low over little clay paths and the burrows that other children have made. Cubbyhouses, some modelled on the gunyahs their teacher showed them in a picture last year – lean-tos made of foraged branches and abandoned sheets of tin and fibro that Aborigines like to live in. You know never to enter another kid's cubby, not without being invited. Kerrie and Tommy pass them enviously. They don't have a cubby of their own.

They climb to the higher section that overlooks the aerodrome. A wire fence separates the bush from the mown area beyond the runways. A little plane comes in to land.

'Cessna,' Tommy says and when Kerrie doesn't answer he turns to her and says, 'My uncle works at de Havilland's on Milperra Road.'

Tommy's father works in the city, at a printer in Ultimo. Kerrie has heard her mother and father talking about him. He's a bit of a boozer, Dad said. He likes to set sail on an amber sea. Her dad works at a factory in Yenora, a bus and a train and a bus ride every day, though sometimes he gets a lift with a friend.

Kip starts to bark. 'Rabbit,' Tommy shouts.

Trixie is shivering all over. 'Go on, Trixie, go,' Kerrie says but the dog stays beside her.

They walk over to the indentation the kids call the lake. It's hardly that, just a low place where rainwater gathers, but if you close your eyes it becomes as big and shimmering as one of the Canadian lakes on the map in their classroom. Today the water is thin and the cracked mud on the bottom is showing through it. A waterhen is optimistically picking at some weeds and it's this that has excited Kip.

'Go, boy!' Tommy shouts as Kip lunges at the bird. It dashes into some bushes. Tommy laughs, slapping his thighs. Kip runs back with a dog grin on his face, his tongue and mouth muddy.

Some big boys are walking along the ridge towards them. They carry guns.

When they can see Kerrie and Tommy they raise their guns at them.

'Crikey,' Tommy says, but he stands still, Kip looking up at him thoughtfully, then back at the boys. The hair has risen along Kip's spine.

'Sit, Trixie,' Kerrie says. The boys approach, their guns lowered now.

'What are you doing?' Tommy shouts.

'Hunting, what do you think?'

'Can I see?' Tommy reaches for the biggest boy's gun. He takes it and raises it to his shoulder. Another little plane is landing. Its wheels and the numbers on the lower sides of the wings are just visible. Tommy pretends to shoot the plane down. 'Pop, pop.'

One of the big boys looks hard at Kerrie. 'She your sister?'

Tommy still has the gun pointed at the plane. 'Pop, pop. No. She's my friend.'

'What's your name?' the boy asks Kerrie.

'Why?'

'Just wondered.'

She looks down at Trixie. The mud has given her a brown behind. 'Are we going, Tommy?'

'In a minute.' He hands the gun back. On its hand piece are three letters. A.R.S.

'What are they for?' Kerrie asks. 'Is that your name?' The smaller of the boys grins. 'Yeah, he's an arse.'

The bigger boy cuffs him on the head, says, 'Sure. My name is arse. Want to show me yours?'

Kerrie looks towards Tommy but he's laughing as well.

'How old are you?' the big boy asks.

'Twelve.'

'Pity, eh,' he says to his mate.

'Yeah. See you.' The boys walk away.

Kerrie and Tommy play at the water's edge till the boys have disappeared.

Kip and Trixie chase each other now the waterhen has gone. 'What does A.R.S mean?' Kerrie asks.

'You've really never heard it?'

'No.'

'It means your arse. Your backside.'

'True?'

'Yeah.'

'So how come he's got it on his gun?'

'It's probably his name, Dumbo. Initials. Alan Richard Smith or something like that.'

A crow calls from the branch of a big old gum, *Baaa Baaa*, a sheep sound. Tommy gives his watch a pat. 'We'd better go. It's nearly five.'

They turn towards Edgar Street again, the dogs following slowly, then, to their right they see a neat burrow under some bushes.

'Wow. Look at that. I've never seen it before.' Tommy is already at the entrance, looking in, and then he's down on his knees and crawling towards the back.

'I thought we weren't supposed to go into other people's cubbies?'

'No one's here. Hey. This is the best one I've ever seen.'

Bending low, Kerrie enters the space too. It's lined with neat woven branches topped with bark. The floor is spread with dried grass. A billy can and an empty packet of Craven A are partly hidden by a rock.

'I've never seen one like this before either,' she says. 'This is a grown-up's cubby.'

'It might be. Maybe it's Black Charlie's?'

'Don't be silly, that's just a story.'

'It isn't. He was an Aborigine who lived here a long time ago.' Tommy is stretched out along the floor, his feet sticking outside. The dogs have flopped down at the cubby's entrance. Kerrie lies down too. Above their heads the thatch lets in pinpricks of light. When she's looked through her straw hat at the beach she's seen similar stars and suns. Tommy puts his hand on her thigh.

'You really never heard of an arse?'

'No, never.'

'What do you call it then?'

She thinks for a moment. A bottom? A bum? No, Dad would never let her say bum.

The crow outside is still making sheep sounds. From the distance comes the retort of a gun.

'You ever kissed a boy?' Tommy says.

'No.'

'You ever seen one?'

The question seems silly. 'Yeah,' she says.

'You've seen a boy's you-know-what?' Tommy is sitting up on his elbow. His hand touches the front of his pants.

The cubby is suddenly hot and very small. Tommy has lifted his bottom off the floor and pulled his shorts down. His underpants are pulled down too so that from where Kerrie is lying she can only see the white nakedness of his bottom and the crack that separates the two cheeks. He turns towards her.

'See?'

She looks again at the roof. It's just like the woven basket the baby Moses was put in when he was hidden in the bulrushes.

'See,' Tommy says again and she lowers her eyes to the funny pink grub in his hands.

'Yeah,' she says.

Tommy pulls up his pants and shorts. 'Now show me yours.'

'What?'

'I showed you mine, go on.'

She wants to say 'But I don't have one,' but after the A.R.S. joke she decides it's better to say nothing at all.

Tommy's hands are tugging at the elastic of her shorts. 'Come on.'

She is glad Trixie isn't looking. She pulls down her shorts, then her knickers, and straightens her legs. Tommy's face is locked in concentration and comparison.

'You don't have hair.'

149

'Hair?'

His finger touches her skin and she flinches. He is looking more closely now; she can feel his breath on her skin. Then tentatively he runs his finger along her crack.

'Don't,' she says, sitting up. The dogs sit up suddenly too, ready to go.

They clip the dogs onto their leads and walk slowly to Edgar Street, stopping at the street's high point and turning towards the city. A gap in the clouds has let a ray of sun through and it catches the very top of the Harbour Bridge's arch.

'Look,' Tommy points.

'The bridge,' Kerrie sighs.

A silence accompanies them all the way home. They walk past the new houses, past Gracie's corner shop, not stopping for any lollies or a Paddle Pop.

'Will you come with me again next Saturday?' Tommy asks when they get to her front gate.

'Yeah.'

'Okay. See you.'

'See you. Come on, Trixie.' She pulls the dog down the garden path. As soon as she's off her lead Trixie flops down onto the kitchen floor as though she feels weary too.

Dad looks up from his paper. 'Here's our little Kerrie,' he says. 'Have you been dreaming about that house by the bridge again?' His legs are pale and freckled and the late sun catches the ginger hairs on them. 'Put the kettle on, pet.'

She turns to fill it, grateful for the scent of the match as it ignites the gas, of the tea in its canister and the sweet biscuit smell of orange creams. She is a small and frightened thing now, and she is suddenly grateful for the small, safe, domestic rituals of a girl. Trixie sighs, rolls, the pink line of the scar where she was desexed visible under her white fur. She and Trixie will walk in another direction next week, Kerrie decides. She will find new friends and leave Tommy to find his own.

A Funny Story to Relieve the Tedium of Reality

Above the clatter of knives and forks on plates, Penny said, 'I'm dying to tell you a funny story. It was told to me by a friend in confidence, so I've changed all the names. Don't ask me who told it, okay? Just go with it.'

'Funny peculiar or funny ha ha?' her husband, Tim, asked.

'A bit of both really.' She paused for effect and looked down the table at me. 'And John, I don't want you to take it, okay?'

Everyone else at the dinner table looked at me too. 'Take it?' I said.

'Yes, you know, steal it. I don't want to find it in a book one day. Because if you use it the friend who told me, in confidence, about *her* friend, will know I told you. I'd never be able to face her again if that happened.'

'Okay, Penny,' I said.

Someone reached for the decanter of wine. Tim is a wine buff so we don't drink red wine from the bottle anymore. The decanter rang a pure crystal note against a wineglass. It sounded like a tuning fork. I expected everyone around the table to hum.

'Right.' Penny gave me a little smile and settled back in her chair. 'My friend's friend' – she was sticking with the no-names rule, I noted, so there was no way of knowing who these people were or whether we were acquainted with them – 'told this story in the pub the other night. She'd been watching one of those family-tree programs you see on TV. Do any of you watch them? No, me neither. Anyway...'

I couldn't help but ask a question. 'How old is this person?'

Penny looked annoyed. 'Which one?'

'Not the person telling the story in the pub, the other one, the friend's friend.'

'I don't know. Sixty, sixty-two.'

'That old?' Liam said.

'It's not *that* old. My mother's that age.' That was Monica.

'Are we all ready now?' Penny gets a chill note in her voice whenever she's pissed off. I could already hear the iciness creeping in so I sipped my wine and the others did the same.

'Well, my friend's friend was looking into her family tree and she discovered that her great-aunt Flora, who only ever had one child——'

'A boy or a girl?' I asked.

'A boy.'

'Right.'

'Well, this boy had been adopted during the war.'

'That happened a lot,' Monica said, 'especially if women got pregnant while their husbands were away and they couldn't possibly be the fathers.'

'Lots of randy American servicemen, I've heard,' said Tim.

Penny cast him a withering look. 'Shall I go on?'

'Sorry, sweetie.' Tim looked around the table and, noticing my glass was empty, raised the decanter quizzically. I shook my head and pantomimed driving a car.

'Okay. So Aunt Flora went up to Liverpool to see a friend. She was going to stay a week but ended up staying for three months. When she came back to London she had a baby with her. All her friends and family were shocked. She said it was hers. She hadn't wanted to tell them she was pregnant before she went and decided to surprise them when she got back.'

'She must have shown something.' Monica patted her stomach. 'It's pretty hard to hide a pregnancy, especially if she was in her sixth month.'

'That's the point,' Penny said. 'Everyone knew she was lying.'

Annette interjected. 'She mightn't have been. My sister, Kim, barely showed at all through her pregnancy. She worked right up to the birth.'

Penny gave Annette a withering look. 'Well, your sister is a miracle woman, isn't she? How many companies is she on the boards of now?'

'Only three, Penny.'

Liam nodded and sighed. 'Kim's pretty wonderful. Is she still doing marathons?'

Annette nodded.

'I rest my case,' Penny said. 'Does anyone want to hear this story?'

'I do.' My curiosity was rising inside me like proving bread dough.

'You promised, though, right? You won't use it?

I drew my fingers across my mouth, zipping it. Penny has distrusted me since I wrote a short story in which the male character had an affair with a woman whose family owned a restaurant in Brick Lane. The character lived in a house just like Penny and Tim's, same street, same kitchen designer. When it was published I explained that it wasn't about them. Tim is as faithful as an old Labrador, God knows why. Penny would cut his balls off if he wasn't, I suppose. I didn't think that the appropriation of top-end appliances and Stromboli volcanic downlights would cause much distress, but Penny disagreed.

'They had sex on my granite benchtops, John, surely you didn't think I'd approve of that?'

Since then I've been more careful with disguise. I use the kitchens from glossy magazines now.

'Right, where was I?'

'The woman has just come home from Liverpool with a baby she said was hers but the family decided wasn't,' I said.

'That's right. It didn't take long before word spread. That little lad of...well, he's not her lad at all.'

'That seems very unkind,' Monica said. 'I mean, really. What were those people thinking? During a war every little kindness is a good thing, surely? She did the right thing in taking someone's unwanted child.'

Penny shrugged. 'It's not my story. I'm just telling you what my friend told me her friend told her.'

'Where was her husband while all this was going on?'

'He was at home, Liam. He'd had to stay in London because he was working for an essential service, I don't know which one, but he was overjoyed with the baby. He and his wife had been trying for years and now he had a son.'

'Hold on a sec,' Tim said. 'Let me get the cheeseboard.' He stacked the dirty dinner plates and took them away and came back with the board and put it in the middle of the table. We reached over, one after the other and cut ourselves some cheese while Penny looked on. When we were all settled, she started again.

'They survived the war and in 1945 when the little boy was four years old, they went up to Manchester to live. The woman had relatives there and they found her husband a job in manufacturing. The question mark over the boy's origins never disappeared, though, especially as he had lovely golden curls and blue eyes, and the woman and her husband were both dark-haired and brown-eyed.'

'Could have been a throwback gene,' said Liam. 'Look at the Bernardis who run the gelato place up the road. They're Sicilians and their three sons seem to reflect the various waves of Sicilian history. One son looks Arabic, the other could be an ancient Greek statue and the third, the youngest one, well, he could be a Norman.'

'I've never noticed that,' Monica said. 'You saw *all* that when you went in there to buy gelato?'

'Yes, I did.'

'Clever you.' Penny's face was pink. She was drunk, I realised.

'I want to know what happened to the family in the story. Was the baby really hers? Was it adopted?'

'Promise you won't write this into a story?'

'I've promised, haven't I?' I said impatiently. How many times did she need to be told? Do writers always have to be treated like thieves?

'Well, they kept up the lie for about sixteen years. Then, just before his seventeenth birthday the boy got his girlfriend pregnant and he went to tell his mother. She lost her temper and said something awful like, "I should have known you'd come to no good with a family background like yours." The son was horrified. He wasn't a fool. He'd heard the rumours all his life too. People are so insensitive, they don't think kids listen. But he had. He'd taken it all in. He'd even asked her on several occasions if any of it was true and she'd always reassured him. "No, of course you're mine," she'd said, and he'd believed her.'

'More fool him.'

'That's unkind, John. I thought you were nicer than that.'

I just wanted the story told. I wanted to know who the man's birth parents were and what he did when he found out the truth. Did he go looking for them? Did he find them? And what happened to this new generation of unwanted children? Did the boy marry his girlfriend? Did he reconcile himself to his history?

We moved on to dessert and coffee. The conversation had veered away from the little golden-haired boy who became a randy and careless adolescent – it was now all about Corbyn and Cameron and UKIP. But before we left I was determined to meet the older man, the father and adopted son. I wanted to hear what he made of his life.

Penny was sipping a dessert wine, some Monbazillac from the crate she and Tim had brought back last summer from a visit to their holiday house in the Dordogne. Liam is always happiest talking politics and I could see from the look on Penny's face that she was displeased that he was hogging the floor. The spotlight had gone from her and her recycled story. I was the only one interested in hearing the ending. If I pushed too hard she wouldn't tell me what happened because she'd think I was going to steal it. If I seemed indifferent she wouldn't tell me either. In her eyes I'd be just like the rest of the overfed drunks around her table. Like them, I'd have lost interest in her human-interest story and moved on to dull politics too.

I decided to take a new tack. I waited until we were all leaving, making enough racket to wake the whole street, and I whispered in Penny's ear as I kissed her. 'You're a great storyteller. Will you tell me the rest of it if I call you next week?'

Penny kissed me back, her breath hot and Monbazillac-sweet as it grazed my face.

'Only if you promise…'

'I promise, really. I promise not to steal it.'

I didn't ring Penny the next day or the next. I went up to Liverpool the following weekend to catch up with an old friend who teaches music at the university. We met for lunch at a pub near the Tate and afterwards we walked along the Mersey, our conversation punctuated by Gerry Marsden as the tourist ferries slid past.

'Jesus,' I said. 'Do they play "Ferry Cross the Mersey" every time they cross the river?'

Stephen was so used to the din he'd not even noticed. 'Oh, yes,' he said when he realised I'd been talking to him. 'Ad infinitum. Sometimes I hear it inside my head when I'm trying to concentrate on Berlioz.'

While Stephen went into a public toilet I stood looking downstream towards the river's mouth. The water was moving fast, and seagulls, wide of wing and raucous, were gliding in the air currents above it. I imagined how this part of Liverpool must have looked during the war, the city's powerful industries and shipping consumed in the war effort. Had the woman in Penny's story come here to gaze at the Mersey, contemplating the important step she was about to take and the deception she'd need to pursue to pull it off? Did she bring the baby with her before she caught the train back to London?

'What are you looking at?' Stephen said.

'The Liver birds.'

We tilted our heads back and stared up at the bronze birds for a while, then decided there was time for another beer before I caught the train to Euston. We walked back to Lime Street deep in our own thoughts, Stephen's on musical composition, no doubt, mine on the woman and baby.

It was the Wednesday of the following week when I finally rang Penny. I caught her just as she was coming home from picking the kids up from school. I could hear them running helter-skelter around the kitchen. Penny was shouting about crumpets or cake and a small piping child's voice answered.

'Crumpets and honey,' I said. 'That takes me back.'

'Crumpets and Marmite,' she laughed. 'Alfie is a barbarian.'

'Will you finish the story for me?'

'You really are keen.'

'Who wouldn't be? It's a great yarn.'

'I'll need to wait till after dinner when the kids are in bed.'

'Better still, why don't I take you to lunch? Tomorrow?'

'I can't tomorrow.'

'Friday, then?'

'Okay. Friday,' and she named a cafe in Spitalfields.

Penny arrived before me, which wasn't conducive to a good mood. She liked to make an entrance, I realised too late. I should have been in place for it. Instead I walked over to a sullen table. 'Sorry. Tube.'

She shrugged. The story of the woman already felt like a kite straining on a rope. Any moment now the string might snap and the story would be irretrievably lost. The food and wine helped, though. After the entrée Penny relaxed and we were off.

'The boy went looking for his real parents but he never found them. What is really off, though, is that his girlfriend allowed his mother to keep their little girl and to bring her up as the boy's sister.'

By the main course I'd got the full picture.

Penny picked at her duck. 'The boy and his girlfriend eventually married and had more kids but their first child, now known as his "sister", was never told the truth. She remained with her grandparents and believed they were her parents until…'

A waiter arrived at the table and began to clear away the plates. 'Dessert?' he asked and when I nodded he brought over a menu. Penny took ages to decide, the waiter hovering in case she needed some help. The story hovered too, tantalisingly: a boy, his girlfriend, their baby who turned into a sister, and her adoptive grandparents.

At last he was gone and I sat back in anticipation. 'And then?' I asked.

'And then? The grandparents died within months of one another, the woman first, then the man. All the birth certificates were discovered with the old man's will. It was all meticulously in order. No skerrick of information was withheld. They all found out the truth and dealt with it, I suppose.'

'What happened to them all?'

'I don't know. My friend didn't tell me that.'

I snorted with disgust and tossed my serviette onto the table. 'You're joking.'

'No. Why? It's enough of a story in its own right, isn't it?'

'Well, no, not really. A story needs a conclusion and preferably a happy one. Stories relieve the tedium of reality. They need a denouement to cheer the reader up.'

'You sound like a university lecturer, John, one of those creative writing professors who offer courses in *The Guardian*. There's no need to get annoyed about it. I've told you all I know.'

Penny's story stayed with me for months. I kept seeing the furtive woman on her way north to adopt a child. Was she wearing the severe make-do clothes of the war? Sensible shoes, a suit recycled from the parlour curtains? Where did she go in Liverpool to collect her boy? Who was the mother who gave up her child and how did she feel as she watched another woman take him away? Or was it nastier than that? Was he like one of those stolen kids who were sent from Liverpool to Australia or Canada and their parents never found them again?

Worst of all, I couldn't stop thinking about the knowing family and friends who wouldn't leave the deception alone. They were a Greek chorus in my mind's eye, as harsh-faced and unforgiving as peasants in a medieval painting. I could hear them whispering – 'How dare this woman think she could pretend to motherhood.' And as for the boy, the adolescent father who must have watched in a kind of agony as his daughter was brought into a new iteration of the lie, what did he make of the life his daughter had been given? Where was he now, and where were his children and grandchildren? Had the thread ever broken? Had they cut themselves loose from the folly of a past where parenthood became a game of chance, of broken dreams and broken promises?

I broke my promise to Penny. I couldn't help it.

I began a novel and on the opening page a young woman and her older husband were walking along the platform at Euston. It was 1941. The young woman had a little battered suitcase and she entered a second-class compartment and leaned out the door. I saw it through a black-and-white misty fog of steam trains and cigarette smoke. The man looked like Trevor Howard and the woman like Celia Johnson. The novel ended around a dinner table forty years later as an adopted man celebrated with his extended family.

There were too many of them to fit around the main table so the children were seated at a separate table in the kitchen from where their parents could occasionally hear squealing. One or the other of the adults would get up to investigate and come back shaking their head and laughing. The man had discovered that his birth mother and her siblings had been killed when a German bomb hit their terrace house in Toxteth. He'd grieved them for a while but also felt blessed that he'd been spared the same fate.

I gave my story a happy ending because I couldn't imagine what else to do with it. I'd had a happy childhood. My adolescence had been uneventful. I had the man tell his daughter the truth. She was fifteen by then and he didn't want her to discover the truth, as he had, on the portal of adulthood. His adoptive mother, well, she forgave them all. They all lived happily ever after, or as happily as anyone can expect to live these days.

When the novel was published Penny didn't speak to me for months, though the other friends at the table could see why I'd broken my promise. The adopted man needed an opportunity to tell his story to his sister/daughter to set the matter right. If he didn't, the gossips and malicious storytellers would have won the day. What lies could they have told his daughter? What ridiculous embellishments and fictions might they have made of the whole story? It was his life, after all. If he had any right to it he also had a responsibility to set it straight.

I justified my appropriation to Penny with the idea that the world has become so dishonest that writers have an even greater responsibility to tell the truth, even if it's all a fiction. She just huffed at that. She'd told me a story at her dinner party, I said, and in so doing had opened a door and pushed a little character into my path. That little kid had offered me his hand and I'd taken it.

Writers have no choice but to offer truth a refuge in our stories. We have no reason to exist other than to tell stories: funny, serious, true, fabricated. A story is a place where truth and the imagination work together to create emotional and artistic meaning – its truth and promise in dialogue, I guess. In that role I find myself talking back to politicians on the TV an awful lot more these days: 'I'm a writer and for the sake of a story I break my promises,' I say. 'What's your excuse?'

Going to Visit Dad

The car's indicator made a dull, hollow sound as Pete turned into the driveway. Sunnyholme. He drove straight into the visitors' area. The sky was a pale, flat grey, some clouds close to the head like a caul. He sighed as he eased the car into its parking spot and opened the window for a moment to let in some air. It smelled metallic, like rain on a hot tin roof. A nearby church bell was ringing in a dull, languorous tone. When he'd visited his father last week the sky had been blue and he'd wondered how long the unseasonable weather would last. Early May and people still in shirtsleeves? It had to be global warming. Winter's breath was on today's air, though, announcing the summer was gone.

Not that the warm weather hadn't been appreciated. Last week he'd taken his father out into Sunnyholme's neat garden and they'd sat, side by side, in the sunshine amongst the late-flowering roses and daisies. Sunlight had been latticed across the lawn and he'd kept glancing sideways at his father's frailty, the way his hands had become ropy and bent. His voice had become soft too, and tentative; he was becoming more confused about where he was. Pete had talked at his father loudly in the jocular voice people used for old people and little kids. 'Hey, Dad, remember that time we went to Kiama for the day and you thought I was going to run across to the edge of the blowhole?' He smiled at the thought of his young self, that boy in shorts and a t-shirt, knees as dirty as newly harvested potatoes. His father had been right to be concerned. The blowhole huffed its salt spray at them, challenging them to come to its brink, but he'd felt his father's constraining hand on his shoulder and had looked up to see his face misted with salt spray too.

The sea, the sea: so many trips to beaches and blowholes, so many seaside picnics and barbeques. He seemed to shout sea memories whenever he visited his father. He thought his loud voice might penetrate the fog, he supposed, might hook on to and reel in a memory for him. Days at Manly and Austinmer, Kiama and the blowhole: his words metamorphosed into the boom of surf, the white bash of waves on sand, the pull and push of the tide. They'd talked about football last weekend and a trip on the ferry to watch Balmain play Manly at Brookvale Oval. How the Wests Tigers were nearly on top of the league now. The Tigers nearly winning a lot of games this season. Nearly. Not much to be cheerful about today, though. The team had been thrashed by the Roosters yesterday.

He turned off the engine and sat for a while. These visits always took a courage he hadn't thought he possessed. Jollying someone along had never been his forte, those breathless 'remember when's and 'you've got to laugh's and 'what year was that again?' Yet here he was spending most Sundays playing the loud and over-cheerful son, the avid football fan, a man fishing for memories in his father's rapidly emptying pond. Some other visitors pulled in beside his car. They smiled at him as they got out. Italians. He'd seen them here before, spooning homemade pasta into a mother's mouth, sifting through old photos, talking in the cooing way he knew was ahead for his dad.

He waited until the Italians had gone before he got out of his car, stood and stretched. Ellie had packed a little bag of things – a new pair of flannelette pyjamas, a cake of soap, some football magazines and a block of chocolate. She was knitting his father a jumper of teal blue wool, eight ply, with a cabled front. 'I'll be finished in a few weeks,' she said as she *click-clacked* her way through a favourite TV program. 'That will keep your dad cosy through the winter.'

The nursing home was overly warm, so thick jumpers weren't really needed. He hadn't told Ellie that though because she wanted to help his dad and he was grateful for her concern. She always offered to come to the nursing home too, but he preferred his visits solitary. Two precious hours together as his father slipped away from the shoreline of his past; there was something so painful in it he wanted it for himself. It was as if each visit offered a kind of exfoliation, a pain so intense nothing but smoothness could come from it. Just under his old skin he was growing a new metaphor-skin of falling curtains and closing doors and diminishing shorelines and missed catches. 'We'll all confront this one day, so I might as well get the metaphors right for my own old age and death,' he joked to Ellie. There was never real humour in the joke, though. This was awful. Visiting his father scared him to death.

He picked up the bag and straightened the rug on the car's back seat. Once, he'd harboured the idea of taking his father on little drives to those familiar childhood places like Kiama and Manly and the restaurant at Razorback Mountain where they'd often gone for a Sunday roast, or the railway museum at Thirlmere where his father loved to clamber onto all the old steam trains. As a boy he'd enjoyed his father's pleasure in those outings – his parental delight in giving his kids something nice while at the same time behaving like a big kid himself. Places that spoke of a Sydney childhood, of car sickness and coconut oil beaches, of picnic sandwiches and dressing-gowned *Disneyland* on Sunday night TV.

His planned day trips had never eventuated. The nursing home discouraged dementia patients from being taken outside the facility, away from an environment they'd learned to negotiate despite their constantly diminishing mind maps. Even going to the dining room could place an enormous strain on them, the head nurse said. 'They get very upset with themselves – well, with all of us actually – if they can't work out where they are.' So he'd given up that idea. Like the Italian visitors, he brought photos instead.

Pete looked around the car park for his mother's car. Thank God it wasn't here. Last week he'd tried to talk to her again. How long had they been feuding now? Three years? He'd tried to say he was sorry if he'd been a bad son but there had been too much accusation in his voice as he spoke. She'd picked it straight away. 'Bad son' sounded like 'bad mother', though he hadn't intended it to. They shared a concern for a fading man, after all. Surely their old squabbles could be set aside? The past had taken on a new and urgent meaning now his father was losing his. 'Shall we let all the old slights go?' But his mother had accused him of taking his father from her and he'd hung up in a rage. He'd stood by the phone for a moment, half-expecting her to call back. She didn't, but Ellie had heard his raised voice. 'Oh, Pete,' she said, hurrying into the lounge room. 'Just keep going to visit your dad. *He* knows you're there. That's all that matters.'

Mothers, fathers. His own kids seemed uncannily well adjusted. They never fought. They even seemed to like their parents. That was all you could ask, wasn't it? However hard he tried, he couldn't remember when he and his mother first started fighting. He couldn't even recall what their first fight had been about. He'd always felt the burden of her expectations. Be best at school, at sport, at making friends. He'd failed her on all counts. He was his father's son in that regard. His father's credo had always been *Life should be good enough*. Don't stress too much. Get pleasure from what you can. He saw his father in the cabin of an old steam train at Thirlmere again, his face all delight. Pete wanted his own life to be like that: immediate, happy, free from stress. He wasn't quite there yet but he was trying. That was what he and his mother had fought about, he decided, a life struggle between his father's view of the world and hers. He had always made it clear to his mother which team he was on.

It was bloody hard, though. He'd been sitting in the kitchen one weekend not long after the latest altercation with his mother. He'd been flicking through an old photograph album, one in which all the photos seemed to be draining themselves of colour in a rush towards sepia. As he looked at a Christmas tree, underneath which he and his sister sat surrounded by brightly wrapped boxes, he heard Ellie chatting about his mother to a girlfriend on the phone. 'She's a shocker. You'd hate her. She really wants to hurt Peter.'

He didn't see it like that at all. Once his father developed dementia his relationship with his mother became more primal, more competitive, as though they were two Neanderthals fighting over the same bone. As he looked at Sunnyholme's ordered gardens, at the waste bins neatly lined up, not quite out of sight by the utility block, he thought, we're fighting for supremacy, not only over the past but what was left of his father's future. He'd fallen out with his mother because of that, exactly. She wanted everything in the past to be idealised, for the future to be dignified. It would all be neatly managed.

He was more of a realist. Despite their differences early on he'd spoken quietly to her about his father's fading memory and had been shocked by her obdurate denial. She'd been outraged. 'He's fine. Your dad always had a bad memory. Mine's going too.' But his dad hadn't always had a bad memory. It had always been pretty good. He could draw the past to him like a magician, plucking from his top hat memories of the things the family had done ten, twenty, thirty years before, picnics and birthdays and Christmases. He'd loved the family dinners when his father had embroidered the detail into all his stories, his sharp focus and instant recall. But he and his mother had continued to argue repeatedly, his mother only accepting the truth when his dad was found lost and in a distressed state at the local shops. He didn't know his name or where he lived. 'See,' Pete had snapped when he and his mother went to collect him from the kind newsagent who'd settled him down with a magazine and a mug of tea. 'I told you. You might have spared him this.'

So they visited him separately now, his mother going every day except Sunday, Pete assiduously avoiding any contact with her. Occasionally Sunnyholme's nurses acted as mediators. 'Your mother asked you to take these books away,' one had said on his last visit, passing Pete some books he'd left the previous weekend. 'She said your father won't read them.' Even the nurses know, Pete thought as he took the books from her, and when she wasn't looking he put them back in the bottom drawer of his father's bedside locker.

As he walked towards the nursing home's front door he was thinking about making model aeroplanes with his father. He pressed the security button. Those balsa-wood wings and the smell of Tarzan's Grip, the meticulous painting of flags on each wing's underside. Afterwards they'd hang them on fishing lines from Pete's bedroom ceiling and his father would linger with tales of the Dam Busters and the World War II air raids on Germany. He'd learned a lot about history that way, falling asleep to the gently rocking shadow of a tiny spitfire or a Lancaster.

The duty nurse looked up from her desk. Pete had never seen this one before. 'Can I help you?' she asked as he signed the visitors' book.

'Just going to visit my dad.'

She turned the book towards her and when she saw the name she said, 'Oh, but he's gone.'

'What do you mean, he's gone?'

'He went on Thursday.'

'Thursday?'

'Yes, Thursday. Your mother took him to a new facility.'

'A new facility? Where?'

The nurse stood and walked to the filing cabinet and thumbed through the files. She extracted one and read it with her back turned. Pete looked out to the street. He was glad she couldn't see his face. Too many emotions were passing across it: surprise, anger, confusion, grief. Even before she turned back he knew what was coming.

'I'll just go and speak to the manager,' the nurse said and he raised his arm in resignation, not turning round. As he waited he thought, 'I'll kill my mother.' He wanted to barge through Sunnyholme and into his father's room, with its scents of stale urine and talcum powder and over-brewed tea. He wanted to see his father in the armchair by the window, his old tartan dressing-gown barely masking his shrinking body. Every visit there was always a look of recognition, though. Always. His dad would smile when he sat opposite and took out the photos he'd brought. 'Look, Dad. Remember this?' For a moment his father's eyes would take on a panicked look as he reached for the photograph. Pete named each person, explained what they were doing, and just as in childhood storytelling, his father would laugh and join in on all the action. *Christmas. Yes. Manly Beach. Waves,* his arms mimicking the swell and crash of the sea.

'That's right,' he urged, but as soon as his father returned the photo his face went blank and his body slumped, as though all energy, all memory had been stolen by the image.

Someone else has that room now, he thought bitterly. There are waiting lists for places like this.

'Mr Harrison?' A different nurse was at the reception desk.

He stood. He placed the bag of things for his father on the sofa and followed the woman along the corridor to her office.

'Right.' She closed the door. 'I'm Vicki. Has your mother not contacted you about this?'

'No, she hasn't.'

'I see.'

In the silent room he could hear the over-loud TV in the patients' lounge, a game show, all bells and cheering audience.

'Where's my father?'

'Your mother asked that we not pass on his new address.'

'What? But I'm his son.'

'I realise that, but your mother is your father's next of kin. She's his legal guardian and she can decide where he lives and with whom she shares that information.'

Pete looked down at his hands. A slow rage was rising in him. He could feel it in his feet, his calves and thighs. Soon it would reach his chest and when it did his heart would explode.

'Is my mother allowed to do this? Has anyone else ever done such a thing?'

'Yes, she is.'

'But I'm his son. My father looked forward to my visits. I looked forward to them. Do you understand?'

She said kindly, 'I'm very sorry, but I can't do anything about it. As his next of kin your mother is perfectly within her rights.'

He left the bag of gifts for his dad on the sofa by the entrance. The new nurse was back behind the reception desk. He ignored her as she called out, 'Mr Harrison. Mr Harrison, please don't forget your things.' He pressed the security button and let himself out. The garden seemed full of wild things now. The roses were all thorns and the camellia leaves an ominous green. The pink and red camellia flowers offered mocking faces. He was too furious to drive so he sat in the car and called Ellie. She answered on the first ring.

'Dad's gone.'

'Gone?' She sighed deeply into the phone. 'Oh dear, oh no. He's dead?'

'No, he's *gone*. Mum's had him transferred to another place. No one will tell me where.'

'You're kidding.'

'I'm not.'

'Oh, darling, come home as soon as you can.'

He and Ellie talked through the afternoon but they came up with no solutions. What was done was done. What more could he do? At the supermarket they walked up and down the aisles, stopping here, there, to place something in their trolley. Their conversation was hushed and all about his dad. They might try to find him on the internet or contact the Department of Health. A doctor might be able to give them more information. On Monday Pete would take a day off work and he'd visit every government office necessary, a lawyer and the Guardianship Board. As he reached for a tin of pears he even thought about breaking into the home and stealing the file with his father's new address in it.

'Ring your mother,' Ellie said. 'Tell her how hurt you are. How much you love your father and that you want to spend his remaining time with him.'

'Are you kidding? That's the worst thing I could do. She's a sadist. She'd love to know I was suffering. I won't give her the satisfaction. Oh, El, I can't bear the idea of him dying without saying goodbye. My mother might not even tell me about the funeral.'

'Ring your aunt or your cousins. They'll help.'

Despite Ellie's gentle presence, her soft looks and sympathy, his anger festered all afternoon. He couldn't wait to be alone with his rage, to let it prick and score him. When Ellie at last went outside to the garden he picked up the phone. His mother answered. Pete stayed silent. The sound of Ellie's rake rose up from the lawn. A car went past in the street.

'Hello?'

He let his mother's voice enter him. 'Mum, it's Peter,' he said finally.

The phone went dead in his ear. He called again an hour later. By then he'd arranged everything he needed.

'Hello?'

'Mum, we need to talk about Dad. Where has he gone?'

'I'm sorry, the line's breaking up. I can't hear you.'

He looked down at the photos he'd lined up on the kitchen table and began: 'Shelley Beach, 1965.' He looked from the skinny, tanned boy to the man at his side, his dad's swimming trunks baggy on his lean frame. They had been a last-minute purchase at the beach shop.

'I'm sorry. You're breaking up.'

'New bike, Christmas, 1968.' A Malvern Star. Red. Dad was about to push him down the hill. Pete's smile cracked open his face. He was missing a front tooth.

'Peter?'

'Dad's sixtieth birthday party at the rowing club.' That crowd of boozers in silly hats raising glasses of beer and cheap champagne. 'That summer holiday in the shack on Tuggerah Lake.' Once he'd started, Pete couldn't stop. He went through each photo mercilessly, even when he heard his mother's displeased '*tsch*' and the clunk of the phone as she hung up.

'Balmain's Wests Tigers beating North Queensland, thirty to sixteen, in 2005. My graduation. Dad meeting Ellie for the first time.'

Afterwards he made a pot of tea and took a mug outside to Ellie. They drank it in the garden beneath the jacaranda tree his father had planted when they first bought their house. As Pete looked up he remembered when he'd climbed high through the branches of this tree's parent in his father's garden. I will hold on to my father as he was, he decided. Not the husk he's become, his brain as dried-out and webby as one of the tree's seed pods, his memories dust. The body doesn't matter. My mother can't own what makes my father who he was. He was my dad and I am his son. He looked at the way the tree's branches darted this way and that and took solace from them.

Steers

Keith knows this stock route like his skin, sunspots and wrinkles and calluses – a skinscape that does all the talking about an outback life lived tough. He droves the 650 kilometres to the meatworks, returning with a large cheque in a good year, and in bad with barely enough to pay off the men. The sun is dropping though the heat is not. His backside aches from the saddle. He needs some water but is too tired to bother reaching for the water bottle and opening the cap. The earth is a swatch of reds: termite mounds, crushed rocks and boulders, iron drawn up to the surface and dignified by the light of the dropping sun.

The Aboriginal boys, Tom and Aaron, push the steers along slowly. Two hundred animals, their arses swaying, left to right, their tails, some daubed with dried shit, swinging in time with their gait. A great stream of animals like this gives off a hot, sweaty stink. Steam rises above a flowing bulk of dust-caked muscles. They keep their heads low as though examining the ground. A flash of panic, a spooked beast, would send them wildly careening through the bush, one beast, one head, a thunder of hooves.

He turns in the saddle to look back. The ground is excoriated, open to whatever memories you might want to plant. The Aboriginal stockmen read this landscape like a mystic reads a book of puzzles, all hidden symbols and secret signs. They know where the waterholes are hidden under rocks. Where the wind won't blow. Where the spirits of the elders make you welcome, no bad luck, no sorry business.

The heat is getting worse. It's got its own songlines too. The hat pushed onto the back of his head doesn't stop the perspiration from getting into his eyes. Heat up here is open to the landscape. You see it spread across the earth. You feel it coming towards or passing over you like a bloody great tidal wave.

He's never known heat like it anywhere else. Not humid, not dry, but thick with something. Years and years he's been here and it still knocks him about. On the hottest days it's diabolical. Is it as bad as Vietnam's heat? Probably not.

When he got to Saigon it was like someone had bundled and trussed him in a blanket. The jungle was the worst of it. Vietnam's heat liquefied you, cooking you from inside out.

They'll reach the meatworks late the next day. Each steer will be stunned and shackled, will open itself to the meatworker's knife. A line cut from the breastbone to the stomach, innards flopping onto the abattoir floor, the carcass bled out. He watched the process only once. Each steer guided through a network of wooden fences from the corral. When he was waiting to see the Flying Doctor last year he saw an article in a *National Geographic* about an American lady who came up with the idea of creating slow-moving funnels to ease the cattle along. She radicalised the ways that cattle were slaughtered by saving them the realisation of what was waiting at the funnel's end. Some still panicked but by then it was too late. Trapped within the confines of the fence they could only raise their heads, eyes rolling, and holler as they entered the killing line. Of all the workers the bloke on the electric hammer had the worst of it, studding the blundering steer on the forehead, then the fall, the steam and stink of blood and entrails. After five minutes the stench had driven him back out to the split-rail fence. Death in the bright red heat of midday; some crows had been circling in a pitiless sky.

Tom and Aaron are working the perimeter of the herd, one on the left, the other on the right. They communicate with whistles and gestures, to one another and to the dusty red dogs that skirt the herd with them. He admires the careful choreography of it — the dogs, their tongues lolling, eyes rolling towards their masters, down the herd, up to the men on their horses again, awaiting the shrill whistle to send dog after beast. Animals like this can never be bullied. The relationship between man and dog is too much based on the power of shared work. Approval too — one or the other knowing a time will come when orders are given, obeyed, a skilled move acknowledged. He's seen dogs jump up onto the saddle, their claws harming neither horse nor rider. Hardworking dogs turned kittenish for a pat, sitting before the boss in the saddle. Surveying the herd like this, man and dog and horse as one, makes him think of a beast from mythology, a centaur or a Minotaur, like he's seen in books. His best mate in the 5RAR in Vietnam, Ian Linnet, told him about others. A doctor's son, Ian had been to a posh school where they taught the kids such stuff.

He'd laughed at some of Ian's stories. 'Poofta education, mate. Where I come from it's school of the working class. You go to third form then get off your arse and work.'

Keith's horse walks rhythmically, its undulations between his thighs, its mane covered with flies, keeping the pace he likes, measured, far back enough to get a good view of things, familiar enough to recognise the slightest squeeze of thigh demanding greater speed, or less. Like a good dog, a good horse acknowledges tiredness, anger and hunger. It becomes an extension, a lower body part. A cattle dog is a mate. A horse is part of you.

With a triumphant little buck, one of the younger steers makes a break for the scrub. A small animal, all muscle, no fat, it takes a right angle into a stand of saltbush, the whites of its eyes flashing as it turns its head. 'No, you don't,' he mutters. He cracks his whip and Tom swings back, his dog a shadow of the horse, already crouching, waiting for the whistle. Aaron rides up and down the line, keeping the herd in check. The steer is turned around, harried back to the mob.

Keith doesn't call 'nice work', like he would have once. The men know they're good. They don't need him to tell them, but he quickens his pace and stays close to the stragglers.

Herd, horse, landscape drawing long shadows. The last of the day progresses towards nightfall. Dark comes down fast. The earth and rocks are hot; then as the sun sinks, they become very cold. He whistles to Tom and circles his arm above his head. In ten minutes or so they'll be at the night camp. Tom whistles back. The camp is ready. The boys know these things better than he ever will. The fires are lit, the damper is in the bush oven, the stew in the pot. He's really hungry now. For forty years he's been ravenous. He came back from Vietnam hungry for food like roasts and barbeques, king prawns, beer malty in a sweating middy glass. The hunger never left.

He was keen to keep on the move too. He got away from Sydney as fast as he could, to Mt Isa, Broome, Katherine, then out onto a station where stock riding seemed the best work he'd get. You didn't have to talk to anyone for weeks if you didn't want to. But he still thought a lot about Ian. An eastern suburbs boy, blond, nose freckled like an egg.

'When do you get time to surf if you're studying medicine?' he'd asked him.

'There's always time when the surf's up.'

Nearly at the camp, Keith drops back. He wants a moment with this landscape. Not the landscape the Aboriginal blokes have, that thing they were born with, hovering over an earth so genetic words and maps aren't needed. Something else, something grounded in the shock of life and death. The boys are tightening the herd, pulling them into a shape that will funnel into the configuration they need for the night. There's a waterhole at the camp. Some low, salty grasses that offer the cattle a last feed before tomorrow's dawn start. They'll reach the meatworks at midday. Then the killing will start.

'You wanta mugga tea, boss?'

He looks up into Tom's earnest face. 'Yeah, thanks, mate.' He takes the mug, watches Tom walk away, so bow-legged he can see the camp through Tom's legs, as if through an archway or an ancient bloody gate. He looks at the ground at his feet. Emus have been here, some roos too. The cattle will erase all signs of them, though Tom and Aaron will no doubt still see something of the old tracks. He takes a saltbush twig and scratches about, draws a line, a couple of circles, as though he's playing noughts-and-crosses with himself. He finds himself drawing a map of the ridge in Nui Dat.

The Viet Cong were cunning bastards. They'd seen where the Aussies had planted a line of mines, and crept back at night to move them. A few feet one way, a few the other, nimble and light as dancers. The Americans reckoned they got young girls to do it, marking each mine with a twig or a leaf pointing a certain way. When the Aussies came back it was impossible to know what they were walking into. A minefield of uncertainty; you were in too far before you knew it.

'Dinner, boss.'

'Thanks, Aaron.' He stands and walks over to the barbeque, where the cook has browned half-a-dozen steaks. Fried onions, salad. The station bosses know the value of good tucker on a long drove. The men sit in a circle around the fire. The heatwaves turn the darkening sky into an unfurling flag, the first stars listless in the heat.

'We'll get there around midday tomorrow?

Tom is wiping a slice of bread across the meat juice on his plate. 'Yeah, boss.' Later Tom will scour the plate with sand, rinse it by the waterhole. All the plates bear the scars of this process. Each one might be a map of the passing seasons, the landscape marked by the tracks of thousands of doomed cattle.

'Yeah, for sure,' Tom says again. He's rolling a cigarette now between careful, greasy fingers.

Before sleep Keith goes for a stroll away from the camp. He pisses onto some low bushes, listening to the fall of urine onto the soft earth. The men are in their sleeping bags by the fire talking quietly in their own language. The dogs gnaw on bones at the cattle's periphery. One loud sound, one wrong move and they'll be up and circling the herd. As for the cattle, they snort, shift, a couple low. Heat rises from them still. Tom and Aaron are keeping a close eye on them. They're keeping an eye on him too. They think him odd. He talks a lot less than the other bosses. He gives nothing away. He has a secret, or so they think. Let them imagine what they like. You can't give away anything if you've got nothing to give.

They reach the meatworks just before eleven. Already, the cattle have been graded and moved into separate pens. The first group edges forward slowly, nose to tail. They have no idea, not yet, he marvels. He waits till the last of the group is in the run. They'll be working hard in the slaughter room by now, half the herd today, the other half tomorrow, cutting, boning, the floor awash. The last steer is on the ramp. The abattoir workers are visible now, the stunners with their guns. The beast slows. It is breathing heavily. It defecates, its head rolls to one side. It turns towards him as he stands by the rail. Ahead he hears the *thud, thud, thud* of the stun guns, the fall. 'G'aan,' he shouts, 'g'ann!'

He feels the men behind him before they speak. 'We're goin' now, boss.'

'Okay, Tom. I'll see you back there.'

They'll take his horse. After a night in town, he'll fly home with the station owner in his Cessna. The men walk away; he turns back to the cattle. The last group stands in a silent mob. They'll be killed tomorrow. He lights a cigarette, enjoying the small comforts of tobacco and smoke and the warm wooden fence against his skin.

After the war Ian was going to teach him to surf.

'A waste of bloody time, mate.' Keith laughed. 'My balance is shit.'

Ian looked him up and down. 'You think so? I think you've got a great physique, and a lot more balance than you give yourself credit for.'

Kevin's khaki uniform was drenched in sweat. He could feel it running down his spine in rivers. 'Yeah, doc?'

'Yeah. You'll learn all about waves and the sea and what it's capable of. It's magic, I tell you. Surfing will transform you.'

A few days later they were sitting in a bar, sweltering in the Saigon heat, Ian leaning back in his chair. Civvies – Levi's, a white t-shirt. 'It's too fucking hot,' he said.

'You're a wimp, mate.'

Dancing on the bartop were impossibly tiny girls, like kewpie dolls made up. Too-red lips, black lines around their eyes, breastless. They bumped and gyrated to The Animals' 'Boom Boom' while leering nashos ordered overpriced beers as warm as the steamy air, sugary and flat.

'I need the surf. It cools you down like nothing else.' Ian gave him one of his earnest smiles. Kevin could see the medical student in it, practising his bedside manner in the mirror. Not that he needed to practise, not with that easy charm, that mix of confidence that came from being a medical student and a doctor's son. The surfie thing was incongruous. He tried to escape the vision of Ian riding a surfboard, hanging five in a white coat and stethoscope.

'What?' Ian asked.

'What?'

'Yeah, you were grinning like a loony.'

'Just a funny thought, mate.'

'Want to share it?' Ian waved his empty bottle at the barman. Held up two fingers. One of the girls brought the beers over, sequinned bikini, breasts like birds' eggs on her chest.

'You want beer? You want girl?'

'Yes to beer and no girl, thanks.' Ian took the beer.

She waited for a moment. 'Girl?'

'No girl,' Ian said again.

She swore softly in Vietnamese then teetered off on her high heels, her little arse moving from side to side.

'They never give it a rest, do they?' Ian laughed. 'Never.' He stretched back in his chair again. 'What are you going to do when you get home?'

'I mightn't get home. I might end up dead.'

'You won't. You can run too fast.' Ian laughed that laugh again, a kind of elegant North Shore chortle, nothing raucous or loud in it. His movements slow in the heat, he raised his beer bottle in a languid arc from table to mouth.

'And you?' Kevin asked.

'Royal North Shore or RPA, I guess.'

'And specialising in?'

'Oncology.'

'Not gynaecology?'

'That meant to be a joke? I thought you understood me better than that.'

They drank half-a-dozen more beers but didn't get drunk. The heat seemed to make the alcohol evaporate before it could have any effect. They might as well have been drinking water or Coke. When they walked outside they passed some of the bargirls displaying themselves in a doorway that looked like a brothel, pink lantern light and silk swathes in the mildewed window.

'I don't know why they bother,' Ian said. 'They might as well just do it in the bar.'

The Saigon River flowed sluggishly, great wads of water-lily on the surface, rubbish licking at the banks. The touts were out all along the river path and in the low bushes they heard the urgent rustle of sex.

Keith calls the station owner from his motel and organises to meet him at the airstrip the next morning at eight. He stretches out on his bed and tries to sleep but he can feel his horse moving under him again in a dizzy, unfamiliar gait, like sea legs. Lying in the motel's air-conditioned dark he is a sailor who's just sailed over a vast inland sea.

When he and Ian got back to the camp, the mosquitoes were whining, the fallen dry leaves of the rubber trees whispering along the walkways outside. And he remembered the feel of Ian's mouth on his. He'd clipped him across the head with his army hat. 'You keep your mitts off, mate,' he'd said with a laugh.

'I'll teach you to surf.' Ian laughed back.

Kevin's sea thoughts rise up at him again as the Cessna flies north over the stock route.

The owner calls, 'Reckon that's our boys?' and Keith leans over and looks down to where he's pointing.

'Nah, they wouldn't have got this far yet. It's just some brumbies.'

As he watches the measured ways in which the boss fiddles with the plane's controls and gears, he sees again the sergeant and the nasho who knew something about mines moving slowly between each man. 'Step back, corporal,' the sergeant said softly as each place was checked.

An M16 mine took out Ian's groin. 'Jumping Jacks,' they called them. It flew up to remove his dick, his balls, the lower abdomen, the top six inches of his thighs. So much red, someone might have dropped a bunch of red carnations into Ian's lap. Covered in dust and blood. Even thinking about it now makes Keith's ears ring with the explosion.

He froze; all the men did when they realised they were standing in a minefield, some mines like carrot tops just visible above the soil. Ian was screaming. He'd landed on his back. His clothes were burning. Then the screaming gave way to a whimper, silence. They all waited for the sniper's shot in the back or the bang of another mine going off. The Viet Cong must be watching. They'd ambush them. They were sitting ducks. Slowly Ian's blood stopped spurting. It ebbed away into soil so red even the rocks seemed to be drinking it up. The sergeant was shouting. 'Stand still. Don't move.' They didn't need any convincing. You could hear their water canteens knocking against their shaking legs.

Apart from Ian they all got through that one. An Iroquois came. Ian was loaded into his body bag. Keith kept thinking, 'Poor bastard. Ian'll be hot in that.' The men sat opposite one another, silent all the way back to camp.

Flying above a blood-red land, great shifting waves of red dust. The steers they brought down are all dead now, their carcasses ready for processing into steaks and roasts and pet food.

And he sees Ian on his surfboard riding the sea to wherever dream waves go. They break into the souls of the living, Kevin decides, into the souls of those left behind, carrying the dead and the living together on sea spray, the zing of salty water, on great crashing waves that take you on and on and on towards the shore.

My American Friend

My American friend said, 'This place sure is a lot like Santa Barbara.' We were driving down the Princes Highway at the time and I wasn't sure whether she was referring to the car yards on each side of the road – Toyota bunting blue and white, Ford green – or the tall bangalow palms the council had planted on the median strip. Both offered something jaunty to the highway, the palms rustling, the bunting moving languidly back and forth like the Queen's waves. The car yards gave way to the last of the shops that had survived the Borrowilla Mall, their facades dusty and bored.

'It sure does look a lot like Santa Barbara.' She was chewing gum as she spoke. 'Real spooky, ain't it, the way places look the same?'

I'd never been to Santa Barbara, or to Mississippi where my friend lived. I'd never been to America at all but my American friend had travelled everywhere in the States.

'Nothing like a big Florida mobile home to take you places. King-sized bed, a real neat powder room, a kitchen as good as my mom's.'

'Isn't it a bugger to drive?'

'A *bugger*, oh you are *bad*. It's peachy to drive, just peachy.' She chewed towards a service station. 'You got Great South gas stations here?'

'Not that I've ever seen.'

'It's real big in my part of the world.'

'And in Santa Barbara?'

'Why, you know that's up in California, but they sell gas there too.'

'And this place is like that?'

She looked at me and grinned. 'A real lot, Susie, it's real like it.'

I turned left at Harbour Drive and headed for the beach. If my American friend was going to compare us with California I might as well show her our surf. The old fibro houses close to the highway gave way to new developments: Pelican Shores and Dolphin Cove, their gardens planted with more palms.

She read the names out loud. 'Pelican, Dolphin. You see dolphins down here? How about whales? These houses are real pretty too. Look at the size of that one.'

I slowed so we could take in the house. 'You think they have a pool?'

'Seems a bit pointless this close to the beach.'

'Nice, though,' she said, brushing a fly off her arm. 'Real nice to sit by your own pool with a cocktail, a pina colada or a margarita, don't you think?'

We followed the beach for a couple of kilometres, the sea churned into white horses, a haze above the sand. It was school-day quiet, just a lone surfer doing what he could with the low, flat spread of the water, and a woman walking a dog along the coastal bike path.

'You ain't got many people here, have you?'

'Not as many as in Santa Barbara.'

'Hell no, or Mississippi either. How many people live in Australia?'

'I don't know, twenty-two, twenty-three million?'

'That ain't a real lot. There are three hundred and thirteen million of us in the States.'

We turned inland at the end of the beach, making the shift again from big new houses to square fibro ones.

'These look like poor people's houses,' she said. 'Houses black folk would live in, or southern white poor.'

'We don't have poor people in Australia.'

She didn't hear the joke in my voice, just turned her head towards me and said, 'Well, technically we don't have poor people in America either, not so long as they want to work.'

'The meat-processing plant down here closed a year ago,' I said. 'The steelworks closed a few months afterwards. A thousand jobs gone, just like that.' I took my hand off the steering wheel just long enough to click my fingers.

'That's bad,' she said and her chewing gum made a little popping sound.

'Where do you fancy lunch? By the beach? At the mall?'

'We just left the beach.' She jerked her head behind her.

I turned onto the highway and accelerated away from a truck. 'Oh, there's plenty more beach to come.'

And so we made our way through Borrowilla's northern beaches, its centre, then the beaches to the south, the story the same with each: poor people's fibro houses up near the highway; bigger, better brick ones close to the sea.

My friend made me stop in front of one place so she could take a photo of it with her phone.

'You know what we call houses like that in Australia?' I said. 'McMansions.'

She looked at me blankly for a moment, the meaning slowly dawning. 'Like McDonald's? Right? It sure is a fancy house for a place like this.' Her eyes swept the sandy foreshore where a clump of pigface flowered yellow. A couple of old fibro houses survived close to the water and the newer ones seemed to watch them suspiciously, as if questioning their right to the sand. 'If we stopped like this in my home town and took a photo, people'd think we were going to rob 'em.'

'They might shoot us.'

'Maybe. They sure as hell would want to know what we were doing.'

We laughed together oddly as we looked from the old house to the new one.

'Let's eat in the mall,' she said, suddenly. 'I'd like to see what your shops are like.'

Like shops everywhere, I thought. KFC, Starbucks, Krispy Kreme. I hadn't been to America but I'd seen those places on the TV. Had spent my teen years longing to sit in a drug store with a cherry Coke or a lime ice-cream soda. American teenagers seemed to have a lot of fun. Back then the girls wore soft pink cardigans over swirling skirts, bobby sox with neat little shoes. Pumps, sweaters, bobs, bangs. I had no idea what American teenagers wore nowadays but

I supposed that, like here, it involved a bare midriff, some body piercings and a tattoo.

'You reckon I'll find something nice to take home? A nice dress?'

'I'm sure you will. A tiny southern belle like you, all of size six.'

She threw back her head and laughed. 'You are one scary lady, Suzie. What size are you anyway?'

Not a size you'll ever know, I thought, shifting my bottom and hearing the vinyl of the car seat pull away from the sweaty mass of my skirt. 'I stopped worrying about that when I reached size sixteen.'

She popped her gum again and looked out of the window. We'd reached the main street and there were more people about. Australians have a distinctive look, I'd often thought, especially people who live by the sea. The sun ages their skin too early. They walk with the waddling movement of people who live in rubber thongs. They hail one another slowly, lazily. Shopping is just something extra to do in a beachy, recreational lifestyle, especially when you need a break from the sun.

My friend was thinking something similar. She turned to look back at two teenage boys in board shorts, zinc-white noses, their hair straw-yellow and matted. An old woman in bowling whites was crossing the road.

'She a nun?'

'Bowling. Lawn bowls. You play that in Mississippi?'

'Sure, but not dressed like that.'

I drove up the ramp to the car park, found a parking space straight away. 'You brought me luck,' I said. 'Normally I'd be driving around for ages this time of day.'

We settled at a table in the New York Diner. My friend ordered a Reuben bagel. I had a pizza. The coffee was weak and tasteless, all froth and long-life milk. My friend's chatter began to pall after a while. Comparisons between one country and another had never seemed to me to serve much purpose. Why should I care if Australia reminded her of somewhere else? Once, everyone wanted the place to be like England and as a result we have plenty of places named after towns in Britain. There aren't as many named after American towns, but we're working on it. Dallas, Monterey, Carmel, Boston – but I doubted she had a Kissing Point or a Rooty Hill back home.

After lunch we walked back to the car through the Myer ladies' department, giving a wide berth to an old woman talking to herself in a mirror. 'How does this look?' My friend was holding a summer dress against her body. White cotton, pale blue trim. It didn't look good or bad. It was just a frock on a coathanger up against a tiny body.

'Nice,' I said.

She held it in front of her, shook it so it flapped like a flag. She chewed on her lip, put the dress back on the rack. She chose another one, red this time. Repeated the dress–body thing, shaking the new dress as she had the other. Not like a flag, though, more like the dress was a naughty child. She didn't buy anything in the end. We walked out and into the sunshine. At the car she turned and looked back at the mall's facade, at its Kmart, Target, Woolworths and Starbucks signs.

'We've got all these at home.'

'I know,' I said, 'I know.'

When we got home my friend turned on the television. Oprah Winfrey was on with that doctor who seems to know a lot about everything. My friend stretched out on the couch and watched them. She talked to them sometimes too. 'You sure are right about that, Dr Phil. Oprah, honey, that dress is not a good look now you've put on the weight again.'

She fell asleep after that. At five I woke her and suggested a walk.

The escarpment rises up at the end of my street, a great mass of stratified rock that robs the streets below of the last of the afternoon sun. As we walked, our shadows were cast long before us, turning the grey asphalt a curious blue. I felt as though I was walking through water. My friend seemed to think the same. She stopped a few times to peer down.

'What's making the path shine like that?'

'Quartz,' I said. 'It's in the concrete.'

'It's real pretty. I feel like Dorothy on the yellow brick road.'

When we reached the reserve we followed the bush track up and up, my friend stopping to adjust her sandal straps when the going got rough. We sat to catch our breath halfway up, the sea below like a sequinned throw, the colour shifting from aquamarine to bright blue, a strip of navy announcing the end of the rock platform and the deeper water beyond.

'It is real pretty here,' she said. 'Thanks for letting me stay.'

'My pleasure, it's nice to be able to share it, even if it is a lot like your home.'

'Oh, that's no problem at all. It's not *that* much like it.'

I'll bet it isn't, I thought.

'Do you ever wonder what your life might have been like in another country?'

I didn't answer straight away. At my feet some ants were marching in an industrious line, the lead ant transporting a sizeable crumb of bread.

'Not often. Why, do you?'

'I used to, but not now. Canada. Australia. They're the only places in the world I reckon are anything like the States. I don't think the Europeans think like us at all.'

'What about the English?'

She snorted. 'Heck, I don't get them and their sarcasm.'

The majesty of the escarpment loomed over us. Soon the light would fade altogether. 'There are some Aboriginal rock paintings further up the cliff,' I said. 'It's too late now but perhaps we could go and see them before you leave?'

'I'd like that.'

'Let's go back. I'll fire up the barbeque. We can cook the fish I bought yesterday.'

She stretched, her hands in the small of her back, her impossibly skinny legs browner now than when she'd first arrived. She looked down at the sea, at the ribboned highway, at the old and new houses hugging the sand.

'It really isn't like Santa Barbara at all,' she said. 'It's like nothing I've ever seen before. Nice, though. Real nice.'

And I thought, that's why people want to come here. We're a land of comparisons. Like this, like that. I'll bet for most of the migrants, however much they compare, it's a hell of a lot better than what they left behind. I mean, what's Bosnia or Iraq or Syria got in common with the south coast?

My friend seemed to be thinking along the same lines. 'We're lucky, aren't we?'

'Yeah,' I said, 'we certainly are.'

We walked slowly down the escarpment path. Some joggers passed us on their way up, muscular, puffing. My friend turned around to watch them. I looked carefully and closely at the sea and the shadows and the bush, because before my friend came I'd stopped seeing them clearly. The ancient rocks and caves and paintings had receded under the thin veneer of shopping malls and big, flash houses that had coated the past with the belief of ownership. Stolen, that's what our countries had in common, and, as with all stolen things, the thieves didn't want anyone else to share them. They certainly didn't here and I suppose they didn't in Santa Barbara, either.

'When you come to Mississippi,' she said, 'I'll take you to see the sights. We don't have this' – she turned towards the sea again, darker now, the dropping sun making a long silver thread of the horizon – 'but we sure have lots that's real pretty.'

Snakes of the World

There were four of us once: my brother Nicholas, my two sisters, Petra and Margaret, and me. We lived in an Edwardian villa not far from the sea. Someone had dubbed the house Dowager. The name stuck and my father called the turret on the left side of the roof the house's dowager's hump. We joked about the house and its turret with my father most evenings, when we went to meet him as he came home from the city. Men still wore the city's uniform back then and as his train pulled into the station each compartment door would fly open, even before the train had stopped, and from each one would step a man dressed just like Father, in striped trousers, black jacket and a bowler hat. If Nicholas or Petra had come to the station with me – Meg never did, she was always far too busy with homework or piano practice to come outside – we'd call out 'Father, Father,' and he'd pretend not to hear us. He'd walk right past till Nic shouted, 'Daddy! DAD!', and father would cup his hand to his ear and spin around and say, 'My word. Are you here to catch a train?' To which Nic, guileless as he was, would say, 'No. We've come to meet *you.*' Father would bow and take off his hat and say, 'Well, here I am.' Then home we'd walk along the cliff path and through the woods of our neighbour, Mr Bentley, until Dowager, with her oddly shaped turret, rose from behind a dip in the path to greet us.

One evening, as the four of us walked home, Father in front, Nic just behind him, Petra and me making up the rear, we heard an odd slithering sound in the leaf mulch beside the path and stopped to see what it was. Father said it was just the sea rising up to us. The waves pounded against the cliff at that point of the path. I suspected a hedgehog because we'd found a nest of them the previous year from which three tiny baby hoglets emerged, much to Nic's delight. But it was a snake, an adder, and as soon as we saw it we all rushed to Father and clung to him. He had his furled umbrella with him – another necessary element of his city uniform – and he put his briefcase carefully onto the path then extended the umbrella like a sword. The snake stopped. We all hung off Father, who stood at an odd angle with the weight of us behind him. A thick silence fell until, just above our heads, a wood pigeon called to its mate, *woo woo, woo woo*, and from another tree the call was returned. Father leaned forward and with a swoop of his umbrella caught the snake under its belly, hooked it into the air and flung it away from us, towards an old green-trunked oak, and we all squealed and ran home as fast as we could. Father ran too, swinging his briefcase in one hand, his umbrella in the other, and when we reached the front lawn we stopped, bent over from running, all of us laughing noisily. Meg was playing the piano and the notes cascaded from the music room like water falling from a great height. She must have heard us because the music abruptly stopped and after a few minutes the front door opened and she came out. Typically, she didn't ask what we were laughing at. She just stood and watched us then said, 'Shall I tell Mother you're back?' Father straightened and said, 'Yes, please, Meggsy.' Meg hated her pet name but she smiled politely and went inside and we followed, still puffing and laughing and full of wonder at how clever and brave father was.

I have rarely given snakes another thought since then. Father had shown us what to do if we ever encountered one but I never did – not when I was sent to India with my job, nor when I went to Crete after the war to find Nic's grave, or to Australia when Meg and her husband migrated there. Of Dowager and the woods around her nothing remains, nor of my father, mother or Petra. I hadn't anticipated a snake finding me in my house in France, called jokingly in all my postcards to Meg and her daughters Dowager or *la douairière* in French, though perhaps spinster or widow, *veuve*, is a more literal translation.

I discovered my snake under the flowerpot by the kitchen door. I had gone outside to pull up the mint I'd foolishly planted around the base of the potted rose the previous summer. The mint had grown rampantly. Roses don't like things growing around their roots, and certainly not something as intrusive as spearmint. I stood for a moment looking down at the mint spears then I grabbed a handful and gave it a yank. So root-bound was it that it didn't give at all, but the pot lifted off the ground. I saw a movement to the left of my feet and stepped back.

In that stepping back I could hear the pounding sea and smell Bentley's Wood the evening Petra, Nic and I walked home from the station with Father. Nick was chattering about summer holidays, and building sandcastles and swimming at the cove. Buttercups shone star bright amongst clumps of stinging nettles. We often picked buttercup flowers and held them under Nic's chin. The old children's game is probably not played anymore, but we believed that if you held a buttercup under someone's chin and a yellow patch appeared – a reflection from the buttercup's shiny petals – that person must be a butter lover.

The air was felted with the promise of summer. The trees offered a sense of waiting, of something about to happen. Our voices were magnified in the soft light and on each of our backs shadows passed furtively – golden one moment, dark the next, ghost leaves and branches. Nic was talking loudly to Father as he walked before him, a story about his day at school and some teacher or another. He wanted to build a raft. He would make a mermaid out of sand. Father called back over his shoulder from time to time, 'Really? Very good,' though I suspect he barely caught what Nic was saying. Then followed the excitement of the snake and its dispatch.

The driveway and the area to the side of my house in France are covered with gravel. It's a great forewarner of visitors – you can hear their footsteps crunching long before the person reaches the door. Even the neighbour's cat can be heard when he picks his way across the gravel towards me, so delicately I've often wondered whether the stones hurt the pads of his paws. Sometimes the poplars in my neighbour's field rustle and shiver like running water.

The movement I'd seen from the corner of my eye – I'd let go of the mint and the pot had dropped back with a thud – was a snake, not much of it exposed but enough to see it was not happy with being disturbed. Its head was arched, its mouth was open, tongue flickering. I stepped back onto the gravel, then moved towards the open kitchen door. The snake watched me and I watched it, brown, strikingly patterned in citrus-yellow bands, a small elegant head with bright, angry eyes.

Just as in Bentley's Wood the air seemed to harden and solidify and all became silent. I could feel Nic's hand seeking mine, smell the warm black wool of Father's coat. If the wood pigeon I see each day in the apple tree by my pool had called to its mate, *woo woo, woo woo*, as the bird in Bentley's Wood had called all those years ago, I would not have been in any way surprised. The snake and I watched one another for a few minutes then I went inside, straight to the internet. I looked up the snakes of South West France and there it was, a Western Whip Snake. Not venomous: there aren't many poisonous ones here, just a few adders but they are little and plain and stay well away from people. 'Snakes are as scared of us as we are of them,' Father said that long-ago evening as we clustered around Mother to recount our adventure. Meg had gone back to her piano and upstairs she played Schubert loudly.

That night I dreamed I was standing in front of Dowager again. Meg opened the window of the music room and leaned out and said, 'Kitty, can't you hear I'm practising.' I hadn't heard music at all, just the low, throaty call of wood pigeons, cooing each to each, and the pounding of the sea on the rocks – drums foretelling the war to come. The sound made the evening air feel curved and clear like a fortune-teller's ball. 'Sorry,' I called back. We were always apologising to Meg, and, accepting that as her due, she shut the window emphatically and went back to the piano. I walked along the path to Bentley's Wood and there I found Nic as I'd expected I would. In that sense the dream was a faithful recreation of an incident a few days after our sighting of the snake. Despite being told to keep well away from that section of the path, Nic had gone back to look for it. When I'd come upon him he was thrashing at the brambles and nettles with a stick. His bare legs were pale green in the forest light.

'Nic! What are you doing?' I shouted. He hadn't heard me coming and he dropped the stick guiltily. He walked over to me and took my hand. 'Don't tell, Kitty,' he said. He uttered these exact words in my dream. I said of course I wouldn't and we sat by the cliff path and watched some seabirds diving for fish. The blue and green and turquoise gradations of the sea are still seared in my memory.

For the next few days the snake and I lived together carefully. Each morning I would find her stretched across the gravel and sometimes, if I'd left the hose out, she'd drape her long body across it proprietorially, though I doubt she thought it was another snake. In the heat of the afternoon she retreated to the cool area of her nest behind the pot and if I peered in I saw how artfully she'd continued to arrange gravel and leaves and twigs, and how cool and soft and safe these must have felt against her skin when the sun was uncompromisingly hot. I told my neighbours and they came to peer at her too. They told stories about snakes they'd seen during childhood walks in the nearby *Forêt de la Double* and I told them about Father and Nic and Petra and me and the snake in Bentley's Wood. A week or so later the village shopkeeper told me that nesting snakes would lay eggs and soon my snake would have many snakelets. 'So close to your kitchen too,' she said. 'They will get inside your house.'

'No,' I laughed. 'Surely not?'

As she packed my shopping into a little cardboard box she nodded sagely. 'It might be time to call the firefighters. Let them take your snake to a new place in the forest.'

I thought about this as I sat in my kitchen and ate my lunch. Nic was on my mind again as I spread butter and jam on a piece of still-warm baguette. As far as we could learn he had been killed a few days after his seventeenth birthday and then, not six months later, a bomb dropped from a retreating German bomber as it passed over Kent had killed Father and Mother and Petra, who'd been down from her job at the ministry. Meg was spared because she'd been rehearsing for a concert in London.

As for me, I'd been working at Bletchley Park, a long way from Dowager. The mysteries of code-breaking had

204

appealed to my mathematical side. After Father and Mother and Petra were buried, Meg and I went back to Dowager to claim whatever we could find and neither of us ever went there again. The land was sold in 1952, as was Bentley's Wood, for much needed postwar housing.

I rang the *pompiers* that afternoon and they came in their big red fire-engine. I made them promise not to harm the snake and they assured me she'd be taken to a new place where she could lay her eggs and raise her offspring. They ushered me into my house as though I was very old, then they closed the kitchen door and the outside shutters. I heard the dull thud of spade on gravel – at least that's what I thought it was – and for a horrible, chilling moment I thought they'd cut off my snake's head. But when I came outside one of the firefighters showed me a wooden crate and promised me my snake was in it.

After they'd gone I stood for a long time examining the ravaged nest and the gravel. From where I was standing, looking down, the gravel could have been an ancient landscape with boulders and mountains and ravines, the mint and ivy a long-ago petrified forest, the kind you read about, its trees turned to stone. The shivering poplars could have been the sea, timeless and indifferent. I hoped beyond all things that my snake would be happy in her new place. I took the hose and let the water play onto the mint and its scent rose into the midday sun, as true as memory and as fragile as trust.

The Ring

They were having an argument when he took off his wedding ring and threw it. It hit the wall behind her. She heard it land on the Turkish rug then bounce onto the wooden floor. For a moment the shock of his action silenced them and then she said slowly, 'Jesus, Colin, why did you do that?'

'Because you pissed me off so much, Esther. You left me no choice.'

'There's always a choice.'

'No, there isn't. You leave me nothing.'

He waited for her to say something and when she just looked at him coldly he gave an exasperated huff, turned and went outside. The screen door slapped shut behind him. She looked around the room for the ring. It wasn't on the rug or down by the skirting board. She didn't get down on her knees to look any further. Fuck you, she thought. You chucked it. You can bloody well find it.

The television was playing in the lounge room, one of the ubiquitous crime shows that the ABC screened on Friday nights. They made the weekend seem murderous, as though people had nothing on their minds but killing by the end of the week.

Colin stayed outside in his shed, his little escape warren with walls of tools and a benchtop with vices and grips. He often spent whole days down there repairing something broken, a chair whose legs were weakening, a breadboard split down the grain of the wood. They joked sometimes about the symbolism of it, that the patching-up and sticking together of old objects was a good metaphor for the maintenance of their own ageing bodies.

Esther glanced around the room again for the ring. She didn't wear one because her fingers had fattened over the years and hers no longer fitted. Colin had offered a new one as an anniversary present but she was happy not to bother. She still held on to a residual feminism about weddings and all their symbols. Wearing a wedding ring was like being a cow with a ring through her nose, she and her friends had joked back in the 1970s. Why would she bother getting a new one now? The old one had just been a concession to Colin's romanticism.

Colin certainly loved his, though. It was a gold Irish Claddagh ring, two hands holding a heart on which was balanced a crown, but he'd thrown it a couple of times of late when he was angry and she didn't like that. She didn't like him getting angry whenever she wanted to talk about troublesome, personal things, to leave the room and go outside to his shed or up to the bedroom, slamming the door behind him. She said he should stop 'flouncing' off, aware that the word had pejorative connotations. That only made him angrier and he'd rushed off anyway, no talking, no resolution to whatever problem she'd raised. Talking was nagging however diplomatically she'd tried it. Now she just threw her complaints at him and he threw his wedding ring.

She waited till ten, debating with herself about whether she should walk down the garden to the shed. Tonight was moonless, starless, and the garden was thickly dark. How long would he sulk down there? Another hour? All night? They'd been together so long she should have known better. Let him alone. Just ignore him. Once she would have had no problem letting him fester. She'd head off with her friends. *A woman without a man is like a fish without a bicycle.* They'd all had a t-shirt with that written on it. They all had boyfriends too and some of them married them and surprised themselves by staying married. Forty years – she and Colin held the record, but Katrina and James had been together nearly as long, and Dennis and Libby were coming up to thirty. But it was worse now than when she'd been younger and she could just head out to dinner with girlfriends. Something held her closer to home these days and something bound her more inextricably to Colin. It was funny given that they'd all complained about their husbands back when they were newly married. How they had to always be asked to do things, the rubbish, washing the dishes, noticing the milk was almost gone. As the years passed it became easier to get on with it. 'They'll never change. Just do it yourself,' Katrina and Libby would say over drinks.

Esther heard a noise from the garden, a long, slow groan. It was too close to be Colin in his shed. She walked to the screen door and peered out. A narrow band of light cut across the end of the garden, the light from the shed, a knife-strip through the dark. The sound had come from closer than that. She waited for it again but all she heard was a plane passing in the distance, the roar of it reaching her before she saw the flashing lights on its wings.

She sighed now, a slow exhalation of breath that carried the density of frustration in it. She wanted Colin. She glanced down at the lovely red Turkish rug, hoping for the glint of the ring. The whole room was opulent. Polished. Clean. Her friends paid a cleaner but she never did. Her job was so busy she rarely had time for exercise so the housework became her weekly workout, or so she told herself. Her house was tidy and loved and well repaired. Colin had sanded the old dining table back to life. Everything in the house was old and familiar and cherished. It was just that as she and her friends neared retirement they all seemed to collectively get anxious about letting go of things – the beautiful objects they'd collected, the power of work and the workplace identities they'd carved. Most terrifying of all was spending more time with their husbands.

At eleven Esther turned the television off and peered once again towards the shed. Colin must be feeling the cold down there. The shed would be heaving with spiders and she knew how he hated them. He wasn't going to come inside, though, she could just tell. He'd stay down there sulking until the whole suburb was asleep, the neighbours' lights extinguished one by one, the dark garden closing in on itself like a fern frond. Bugger him, she thought. She checked the door was unlocked, thinking only for a moment about locking Colin out. She decided that would make him all the more angry and she didn't want that. She wanted him to come in as though nothing had happened, as though he'd just been planing away a piece of wood and was happy with the results. She glanced around the room, turned out the lights. Let him creep back in when he was ready.

She didn't hear Colin come in but it was certainly after midnight; that was when she'd tossed her book aside, her ears on the garden. She was tired. She turned off her lamp but got out of bed and switched the hall light on – at least he'd be able to see his way in.

She tossed and turned for a while, thinking about all the years Colin had become angry whenever she'd touched on an uncomfortable emotion, like it was burnt skin, a scab pulled away from something still sore. 'What?' she'd say. 'What have I said that makes you react like this?'

Once, he'd used silence like a drawbridge, like a door slammed in the face. 'When he's like that I could kill him,' she'd said to Libby.

'Tell me about it,' Libby replied. 'They all do it. Women shriek and shout. Men just clam up and make us feel like shrews.'

God. How they'd laughed at that.

Colin came in. She heard him settle on the couch in the study and eventually, it must have been close to dawn, he gave up on the couch and came to bed. Their bodies, like horses knowing the path to their stables, had found their way together despite the fight, and she'd woken to find he was lying with his arms around her, their bodies neatly dovetailed.

She let him sleep on and while she was showering she thought about the only advice she'd really carried through her life from her parents' sixty-year marriage. *Never let the sun go down on your troubles.* She'd said it to Colin when they'd first got together. The saying stuck for decades and then it unstuck because too many times they went to sleep after warring, their grievance unresolved. Whenever this happened she felt they'd betrayed something wise and important, and that they were opening their relationship to bad luck.

She went downstairs to make herself a cup of coffee, hoping the machine wouldn't wake him. She walked carefully, her bare feet and toes instinctively searching for the ring. She was about to sit down on the couch when she spied it in the corner by the stairs. Her first impulse was to take it upstairs, to let Colin wake to the sight of the ring on his pillow, the clasped hands and little heart slowly bleeding into his vision, a forgiving molten gold. She didn't go up. She turned the ring around and around on her palm for a long time, looking at the hands, the heart, the crown, gold-bright in the morning sun.

She thought about the ring for a long time. What a curious thing a circle was. As a child she'd drawn them without the aid of a saucer or bowl, without a compass, until she got hers as right as she could freehand. Another thing accomplished, another example of her self-discipline and drive. The heart and hands grew warm against her skin. Colin's ring carried so much of him in it. He had worn it for forty years with an obsessive commitment that she realised now was as skilful as the circles she'd drawn so exactly when she was a little girl. He had just as exactly demonstrated his commitment to her despite all the challenges. Colin's love was as circular as a ring's. And like a ring he too was forged, shaped, burnished.

Despite these thoughts she still didn't take the ring up to him. Instead, she placed it high on the wall, resting it on a little ledge formed by the decorative wood of the doorframe. It was out of sight but she knew it was there. When Colin came down she made him some breakfast. They said nothing of the ring but while she was washing up she saw him searching the floor of the hallway in case it had bounced against something. They went to the supermarket and afterwards when they were carrying the bags inside she saw him again slow in the hallway, as though the ring might have moved around while they were out. It wasn't there. She caught his eye. Shrugged.

Colin spent the afternoon in his shed and Esther worked in the garden. She clipped a May bush and sprayed some roses for black spot. He was still sanding when she walked over to the shed.

'Would you like a cup of coffee? I'm making one now.' He nodded and followed her through the garden.

While he washed his hands, while the kettle boiled, she went into the lounge room and reached up for the ring. She waited until they were sitting down with their mugs of coffee before she held out her hand and gave him the ring. He took it from her silently and slipped it onto his finger.

He didn't ask where she'd found it or how long she'd kept it from him. He just sipped his coffee thoughtfully then said, 'What would you like to do tomorrow? Do you fancy a day at the beach?'

He'd asked her this, she knew, because he understood how the sea always took her mind off the stresses of work and the hectic week ahead. She took his hand in hers, the wedding ring hard and warm against their skin, and she said, 'That would be very nice. Shall I make us a picnic?'

Plenty

It's Sunday morning and Phoebe listens to the rainbow lorikeets in the gum tree outside, calling to one another in shrill whistles and squeals. There is a particular sound she associates with rain, a three-tone call, *da DA da*, the central note rising before falling again. She likes spying on the birds when they swing from the branches. When one is feeding, the other keeps watch. Head up, neck tense, head down again to the grass seeds and gum nuts. This part of the city is ripe with birds. Even in the early morning light, through the intense blue of the harbour, the rainbow flutter of parrot wing will cut sharply through the background shimmer of water. She is so lucky to live here – all her friends tell her that – to have bought during a downturn in the market, the house worth twice as much now. She rolls over and faces Andy. 'I'm awake, Phoebe,' he says softly. To prove it he moves his arm along the sheet. He will want sex soon. She rolls away, hoping he'll go back to sleep. She must get up. She has a lot to do. Friends are coming to lunch and she has food to prepare.

She makes some coffee and goes out onto the deck to drink it. The harbour stretches before her. Someone might have opened a jewellery box and flung about the stones. The sun catches the new leaf tips of the gum trees along the water's edge. They are like rabbits' ears, like the filmy translucence of a flying ant's wings. She often has her coffee here, looking towards Greenwich, the gum trees and jacarandas spilling down the hillside, some outcrops of yellow rock visible in the balder areas between them.

Andy is up now and has offered to go to the supermarket for some last-minute essentials while she prepares the food. She regards his baggy t-shirt and torn jeans, his sleep-creased cheek. 'You'll change as soon as you get home, won't you?'

He snorts, a sound she has found increasingly irritating of late. When did that start? When he's left for the shops she goes to the fridge and pulls out the chickens. She reaches for the vegetables, the salad greens, tomatoes. There are several small packs of cheese bought yesterday from the shop in the village, the French cheese so expensive it might have been cheaper to take everyone to lunch at a local restaurant.

She is so engrossed in her preparations that she doesn't hear the front door close, just Andy's approaching footsteps and the swish of plastic shopping bags. 'Did you remember the cream?' she calls. She hears a muffled 'shit' and the door opens and closes again. She walks up the hall to where Andy has left the shopping, and rifles through the bags till she finds a bottle of olive oil and takes it into the kitchen. He's bought a brand she doesn't much like. Cheap, it lacks the freshly cut grass taste she looks for in olive oil, something both unguent and tangy, something good enough to dip bread into and savour.

A cookbook is open on the benchtop at a page showing a golden roasted chicken surrounded by lemon halves. She should make the fennel and orange salad now, pretty it with pomegranate jewels just before everyone arrives. There's rocket too, to be dressed with pear and parmesan cheese. Carrie is bringing dessert. She's promised a chocolate roulade. Delia is bringing an entrée, some seafood; she hasn't specified which. She'll see what's on offer at the fish markets, she said. Some prawns, some oysters. Maybe Balmain bugs?

Phoebe asked her to be a bit more specific. How can she plan a lunch when she has no idea what other people are bringing?

'What does it matter?' Andy said. 'Just have some lemons and tartare sauce on hand.' The cream he's gone back to fetch will go with some mangoes Phoebe bought yesterday at a fruit barrow near her office. Some people might prefer fruit, she rationalised, though she knew she'd bought the mangoes because Carrie's desserts are always on the small side. Seven people for lunch and Carrie's roulade is likely to feed five at a pinch. There's cheese beforehand, of course, but you can't expect people to stint on dessert just because Carrie can't calculate quantity.

She hears Andy's key in the door again, his snort as he sees the shopping bags lying where he left them. The bags rustle against each other as he carries them down the hall. He puts them on the benchtop. 'Be careful,' she says. He watches for a while as she pushes slices of lemon between the chickens' flesh and skin. She reaches for the grinder and liberally sprinkles pepper onto the chickens, then crushes salt granules between her fingers, making sure the salt is evenly distributed. The oven has been warming for the past half-hour and she bends to open it, the blast of heat making her eyes water. She rubs her sleeve against them before lifting the baking dish and putting it into the oven.

'Are you doing potatoes with those?' Andy asks.

'No. Why, should I?'

He shrugs. 'I suppose not. They'd be nice, though.'

'I haven't got time now. Salad will have to do. It's not as though we won't have plenty.' She lets her eyes trail across the benchtops where she's arrayed serving plates for the seafood, chicken, salads, cheese, dessert. Elizabeth is sure to bring some chocolates from the specialist shop in Berowra and they'll have them with coffee.

'Shall I set the table?' Andy asks. 'Do you want a cloth or placemats?'

Phoebe looks at the table. She and Andy bought it at Dattner's a couple of years ago. It catches the sun, a rich honey-coloured stretch of recycled kauri pine on a base of red gum. Red gum benches beside the table can seat up to five people each, and the carvers, one at each end of the table, offer something stately and wise to the setting. King and queen, she always thinks when she's dusting them.

'Placemats will do. Use the new white ones.'

While Andy works Phoebe finishes preparing the food, then tidies the benches and goes to change. She puts on a dark blue linen shift. She does her hair, winding it round and round her fingers and pinning it into a knot. She applies perfume, though she's sure she can still smell garlic on her skin.

'You look nice,' Andy says when she comes back into the kitchen.

Phoebe glances around the room again. Not a day has passed since they did the extension without her stopping to admire the way the sun floods into the new glass-roofed room, the lovely golden table standing before French doors that open onto the deck, the kitchen with its bespoke cupboards and pantry and marble benchtops. The splashbacks are mirrors that reflect the room and the garden beyond, so that even when you're at work at the sink you can see the birches along the back fence, their silver under-leaves flashing like fast little fish. She walks over to the table to straighten some of the settings. She places a vase of white roses on the table, some water glasses. Then she stands back. All is ready.

Carrie and James are the first to arrive. Andy has left the front door open and Carrie comes up the hall, holding a large Tupperware container with the dessert in it. Andy likes James and they've already begun their usual banter about wine and cricket and renovations. Phoebe kisses Carrie and calls, 'Hi, James,' because Andy has taken him straight to the stereo to show off some recently bought gadget. Phoebe is always surprised by the way Andy eases into social settings like this. All the men in their circle are like that. She and Carrie and Delia and Elizabeth are more careful with one another, more inclined to distrust. She knows their partners think them odd in this regard – well, Andy certainly does. When did the boys develop their special brand of joking camaraderie? They've all been friends for so long now she can't date it.

She takes Carrie's roulade over to the fridge. 'This looks great,' she calls out, though the dessert is barely visible through its opaque container.

Carrie is pouring herself a glass of water. She turns from the tap and says slowly, 'I hope you like it.' She glances towards the oven. 'Are you making the Jamie Oliver lemon chicken again?'

Phoebe doesn't like the 'again'. She says breezily, 'Yes. I know how much everyone likes it.'

Carrie sets her glass in the sink. 'Has Delia called?'

'No, why? Is everything okay?'

'As far as I know. I just thought she might ring once she got to the fish markets. She's so indecisive, she'll probably need to consult you about what to buy.'

The phone rings just then and Phoebe and Carrie exchange a look, a laugh. 'Told you.'

But it isn't Delia; it's Elizabeth and she's running late. Carrie is following the conversation, and as soon as Phoebe hangs up she says, 'Good old Lizzie. What time will she get here?'

Phoebe has always felt protective of Elizabeth. With a brother like Dan, who wouldn't? All through high school they'd watched as Dan invaded Lizzie's happiness. Everything had to be dropped if Dan needed his sister. Then, at university, when Lizzie was really starting to take off, her poetry getting published in all sorts of journals, Dan would cling to her in the worst kind of way. It always reminded Phoebe of the awful drowning scene in D. H. Lawrence's *Women in Love* when the newlyweds are found with their arms around each other in an awful choking embrace, as though they'd drowned in love, not water. Lizzie's love for her brother had been like that for a long time. Strangling. Destructive. Pointless. He was like an awful narcissistic baby who screamed his need for her until all the air was sucked up;

then he'd disappear again and Lizzie would resume her life, shakily, as if she was punch-drunk.

'She's at Hornsby,' Phoebe says. 'She'll be about an hour.'

They have slipped into the companionable chat of women preparing food. Carrie offers to do the green salad so Phoebe passes her the salad spinner. They hear a car arrive. Carrie goes up the hallway to see who it is.

'It's Delia,' she says.

And here is Delia with two white bags. She kisses Phoebe on the cheek, then Carrie. She hoists the seafood onto the benchtop. 'I bought a kilo of prawns, some oysters and a jar of that red caviar from Tasmania. I hope it's not too much. There are seven of us, right?'

Phoebe bends to peer in at the chickens, which are turning a lovely suntanned brown. 'I'm sure it will get eaten. If not, you can take some home.'

She passes Delia a couple of serving plates. 'Where's Marcus?'

'He had to go over to his parents'. You wouldn't believe what his grandmother has done with his grandfather. Marcus's dad is distraught. Anyway, he'll be here shortly.'

Delia is fanning the oysters outwards from a pile of lemon wedges, an architecture of acid yellow, grey-green shells, milky oyster flesh. She places that platter on the table and empties the bag of prawns onto the other. 'Shall I peel them?' she asks.

Phoebe looks across at her table, its surface vulnerable to spilled lemon juice and prawns and oyster shells. The weight of the house seems to settle heavily on her. 'No, just put out some bowls of water and lemon so people can wash their fingers.'

Andy and James are flipping through Andy's CD collection. Leonard Cohen is singing 'Famous Blue Raincoat'. It's Phoebe's favourite song and she beams across at Andy. She, Carrie and Delia sing along as they continue to prepare the food. Salads, seafood, mangoes, bread. The cheese is arranged on a cheese board and covered with a damp cloth. The chickens are taken from the oven and carved. Phoebe's monotonal kitchen is transformed by all the colour. She looks around the room with a kind of wonder. It is as though the jewelled harbour, the North Shore's verdant trees, the shrieking rainbow parrots have invaded her kitchen and splashed their reds and blues and greens around it. The room seems to groan with the weight of all the food. There's too much, Phoebe thinks.

At last Marcus arrives, followed shortly afterwards by Elizabeth, her cheeks pink as though she has run the last few kilometres.

'Here you are,' Elizabeth says, then, noting the overflowing platters, 'my small contribution.' Her chocolates come in a pretty white box, a turquoise ribbon around it. These are some of the best on offer, made by a woman from Belgium who lives above her little chocolate shop in Berowra. The rich, dark chocolate is coupled with often inexplicable centres, peppered wattleseed, poppy and Pernod, cherry and rosemary. The chocolatier is prone to moments of mad experiment, Elizabeth has said, that's why she loves her produce.

Whenever Elizabeth says *mad*, Phoebe feels her heart shrink. One day Dan will get better, Lizzie says, with new drugs, new treatments. He's being monitored more carefully after what happened when he was in the Riverina, picking fruit.

At last they all sit. They have opened a bottle of champagne and drunk a glass of it on the deck, looking across at the harbour, looking back to the new extension, admiring its architectural elegance, its clever affiliation with the older part of the house. Seated inside now they raise their glasses again. Boy, girl, boy, girl table configuration, no partners next to each other. Phoebe has given Elizabeth the Queen carver chair at the head of the table, a small concession to her being the only single. Lizzie protested, but Phoebe insisted. She has seated herself in the middle of a bench, Marcus on one side, James on the other. The seafood is passed around and they begin to eat.

That evening when she and Andy are preparing for bed, Phoebe tries to recall just when the conversation turned from the food to politics. It wasn't during the seafood. They ate the oysters, large Pacific ones, globular and glistening. James held back his head and let the oyster slide off the shell and down his throat. Carrie did the same. There seemed something prissy in the way she and the others used their forks to lift out the oyster flesh, Phoebe thought, but she preferred it to the self-conscious gesture of tilted head and sliding oyster. She didn't like the way James' Adam's apple rose and fell as he swallowed. It reminded her of a snake swallowing a small animal.

The prawns were sweet and moist and the peeling enhanced the pleasure of eating them. Anticipation, Phoebe decided, some primal food-gathering instinct getting the gastric juices flowing. She noticed that Lizzie didn't bother to strip out the prawns' intestines as the rest of them were doing and she wondered if Lizzie was less inclined to worry about herself and what she ate, or if living on an island surrounded by oyster beds and prawn farmers meant she had a greater knowledge about seafood than the rest of them.

'See,' Delia said breezily as they spread the red caviar onto bread, 'it was a perfect quantity. Plenty for everyone.'

Andy raised his glass and said, 'Thank you, Delia and Marcus, for such a superb entrée.'

No, the subject of refugees was not raised then.

As Phoebe cleared away the first course, the men went outside and Lizzie, Delia and Carrie reset the table with new plates and cutlery. The salads were arranged down the table's centre and the chicken placed in front of Andy for him to serve.

'I love Phoebe's lemon chicken, don't you?' Carrie said to the table and Phoebe detected again the sarcasm in her words.

'God bless Jamie Oliver...and our Phoebe,' Delia laughed and Lizzie said, 'Hear, hear.'

'How's life on that island of yours, Lizzie?' James asked. 'Getting many visitors or do you prefer your solitude?'

Phoebe noticed then how pretty Lizzie looked, the pink cheeks, the shining eyes, the new dress. Lizzie said, 'I enjoy visitors but I also like to be alone so I can write. I've just had a collection of poems accepted by a good poetry publisher. I'm pretty stoked about it.'

Carrie leaned into the table. 'That's wonderful. And how about your brother? He must be thrilled for you.'

A cloud seemed to flit across Lizzie's face. It could have been the shadow of one of the parrots she'd watched earlier, Phoebe thought, brushing against the sky as it turned its somersaults.

'Dan's okay,' Lizzie said. 'I was telling Phoebe about that earlier. He had a job picking fruit for the season. The farmers can't get enough workers, that's why they employ asylum seekers too. It's...' Her voice trailed away.

Phoebe led the discussion along a different route but the conversation seemed to dull; after the seafood, the chicken seemed pale and dull too. The salads did little to raise the dish to the bright festivity of the course that had preceded it. People had stopped eating and their plates were half full. As she rose to prepare the cheese, Phoebe heard Andy say, 'Refugees? Do they let them out to work?' It wasn't a question at all, just a statement followed with one of his little snorts.

Lizzie settled back in her Queen chair. She fiddled with the serviette in her lap. 'Yes, they do, if they have temporary protection visas. It's good for everyone that way. Community respect. Self-respect. People can contribute to the economy.'

Lizzie had always been too earnest for her own good. Perhaps Dan was to blame for that too. She'd learned to be serious from a young age, to defend the ways in which her brother managed to make things go so bad for her. Inappropriate laughter, swearing, wild eyes and filthy outfits – her friends had always avoided him like the plague. Even when he was doing okay, he bore the traces of someone on the edge, a man walking on eggshells, all crackle and terror.

'Queue jumpers?' said James.

'Oh, no. It's not like that at all. These people have temporary protection visas. They want to work and their skills are needed. Dan is really enjoying the work. He's learning a lot about the political situation in Afghanistan and Iraq and Somalia too. It's awful in Syria, so dangerous. It's good, at least, that a few of these people have a safe haven here.'

Phoebe swapped the leftover chicken for the cheese – a breadboard covered with squares and circles and triangles of yellow. There were crackers and muscatels, quince paste, slivers of pear cut so finely she could see the grain of the breadboard through it. She passed around some small plates and asked Andy to pour the red wine.

'What about you, Delia?' Phoebe asked. 'Are you enjoying teaching as much this year?'

Delia laughed. 'Absolutely. The kids are great. I'll never go back to the state system now.'

James was still looking at Lizzie. It was as though he was drawn to her by a string, a cruel puppet master. 'I can't stand the way people think they have a right to just help themselves to this country,' he said.

Carrie said, 'Oh, stop it, James. You're being a bore.'

Delia laughed. 'Yes, let's concentrate on this lovely cheese.' She picked up a knife and pointed to the different offerings. 'What's this one?'

Phoebe said, 'Ossau-Iraty – it's French. It's made from sheep's milk. There's a French Brie, an Époisses, some Comté.'

'I hope you've got something Australian for us, Phoebe,' Andy joked.

'King Island Camembert.' She pointed. 'I hope that appeals to the uber-nationalists amongst you.'

'And you're not?' James said nastily.

'Rather than globalised?' Delia said. 'You *are* being a pain James, really.'

James ignored her. 'Yeah, something like that.'

Lizzie seemed to have shrunk into her chair. She could have been Tenniel's *Alice in Wonderland*, all sulking ink lines, black and white in the still, bright room. James was determined to tease what was fragile in her, Phoebe realised. He wasn't going to stop until Lizzie reacted in some way. She made a face at Andy, hoping he'd rise and join her at the sink, but he just smiled back, raised his glass and said, 'To my lovely Phoebe. Bring on the dessert, my queen.'

James said, 'What do the people of Leeton think about having their jobs taken by foreigners?'

'I understand from my brother that they are grateful for the workers. There's a labour shortage. Australians aren't always available for that kind of work. Country meatworks need workers, so do the fruit orchards. Without them they'd close down and that would be no good for the town.'

'And your brother is qualified to know that, is he?'

Carrie's voice was sharp. 'Oh, shut up, James. Take no notice, Lizzie. He's had way too much to drink.'

Delia laughed and Phoebe was glad when everyone joined her, laughing in a hollow way. 'This reminds me of that scene in James Joyce's *Dubliners*,' Delia said. 'You know. When the family starts fighting at the dinner table. Don't you remember when we all studied it at school?'

Lizzie said softly, 'It's not *Dubliners*, Delia. You're mixing it up with the scene in *The Portrait of the Artist as a Young Man*.'

'Am I?'

'Yes. Don't you remember when they're fighting at the dinner table and the man says, "No God for Ireland! We have had too much God in Ireland. Away with God!" We used to shout it in the corridor between classes, just to annoy the nuns.'

'This is all getting a bit highbrow for me,' said Andy. 'How's your work going, James? Do you think the Aussie dollar will remain strong against the greenback?'

They ate the desserts. Carrie's was as small as Phoebe had anticipated but it was rich and delicious and Phoebe blew her a kiss of appreciation across the table. They drank their coffee out on the deck. By then the sun was sinking beyond a neighbour's Moreton Bay figs, the parrots long gone. They ate Lizzie's chocolates, Andy and James and Marcus drinking a glass of cognac with theirs.

'How is Dan?' Phoebe asked when she saw the men were too busy discussing the cognac to hear.

Lizzie leaned towards her. 'He's up and down. I worry that when he gets sick again the police will shoot him like that poor man on Bondi Beach. But he's certainly better than he's been for a while. He came to see me just before he went north again. I think the move will be very good for him. And you know' – she said this more softly with a quick glance towards James – 'I think meeting some men who have seen awful times and have come here with optimism in their hearts just might have been good for him in some way. Perhaps that might help him to get a greater sense of his own potential.'

'I hope so,' Phoebe said.

Phoebe took a long while to get to sleep. Too much cheese, too many oysters. At least there had been plenty for everyone, not much left over at all bar the chicken. The lunch had gone well, she decided, despite its lurch towards politics. Delia had been right. For a moment there they'd verged on a James Joyce moment – *too much God in Ireland* – trust Lizzie to be able to quote that at them. Well, perhaps there's too much of everything in Australia.

From the harbour came the mournful call of a gull. Phoebe glanced at the illuminated face of her bedside clock. Two o'clock. She was unsurprised. When she couldn't sleep, when she was awake in the congealed night, she often heard seabirds crying in the harbour dark.